FIVE FOR FORTEAU

Kevin Major

The author thanks the people he has come to know in southern Labrador and northern Newfoundland for their kindness and generosity while he went about researching the novel. He celebrates the fifth in the series with the team at Breakwater Books, extending thanks especially to editor Claire Wilkshire for her insight and dedication. Leading lights, every one.

BREAKWATER
P.O. Box 2188, St. John's, NL, Canada, A1C 6E6
WWW.BREAKWATERBOOKS.COM

A CIP CATALOGUE RECORD FOR THIS BOOK IS AVAILABLE FROM LIBRARY AND ARCHIVES CANADA.

COPYRIGHT © 2023 Kevin Major
ISBN 978-1-55081-992-2

We acknowledge the support of the Canada Council for the Arts. We acknowledge the financial support of the Government of Canada and the Government of Newfoundland and Labrador through the Department of Tourism, Culture, Arts and Recreation for our publishing activities. PRINTED AND BOUND IN CANADA.

 Canada Council Conseil des Arts
for the Arts du Canada

Breakwater Books is committed to choosing papers and materials for our books that help to protect our environment. To this end, this book is printed on a recycled paper that is certified by the Forest Stewardship Council®.

high five to the keepers of the light

These people have a blazing passion for lighthouses.

The lure to Point Amour proved more potent than most. At thirty-three metres, the tallest along the entire forty-two thousand kilometres of Canada's Atlantic coast, this tapered monolith has stretched toward the heavens over southern Labrador since 1857.

Constructed of quarried limestone covered by cedar shingles, the tower is painted white, except for a single black band two-thirds of the way to the top. Circling the lighthouse just below its windowed lantern room is a narrow concrete platform, a catwalk. Its iron railing, no more than waist-high, is painted a bright cautionary red.

The catwalk can look treacherous, to the faint of heart. Not so to the undaunted window cleaners, for whom it is merely an access point to keep the beacon at its brightest. For another, though, it proved a point of no return.

She was an ambitious—some now say foolhardy—photographer. She had set out to capture a singular image as the sun was about to shed its final rays for the day onto the intricate arrangement of glass that made up the beacon's Fresnel lens.

Her body smashed mercilessly onto the ground at the tower's base. Blood oozed past the gravel and into the damp earth. Her battered camera lay nearby.

Did the young woman lurch over that railing of her own free will? Did she fall to her death by accident? Or did she die at the hands of someone sharing the catwalk with her?

In the cold light of day will come the answers.

On the Rock (s)
Right On!
Light On!

Labrador

Point Amoor — Red Bay
— Forteau
Blanc Sablon — ~L'Anse aux Meadows
Flower's Cove — ~ St. Anthony
New Ferolle — ~ Croque
~ Conche

Twillingate

Corner Brook —
~ Deer Lake

Newfoundland

~ Cape Bonavista

St. John's
~ Cape Spear

Rose Blanche

Ferryland

Map by S. Sylvester.

St. Vincent's

Cape Race

YOU LIGHT UP MY LIFE

YOU WALK THEM to kindergarten and, before you know it, they're walking across the stage at their high school graduation.

Nick looks to be the proud lad we, the proud parents, have always hoped he would be. (Yes, it's me and ex-wife Samantha sitting congenially next to each other in the auditorium.) Nick does a little shuffle to bring a smile to the face of the principal presenting him with his diploma. She greets him warmly, a sign of just how much he's liked by his teachers. Once he's past her, there's another shuffle and a glance in the general direction of his parents.

He's a bit of a ham, our Nick. He enjoys the attention, though he's careful not to overdo it. He has proved himself to be a hard-working student, at home in what he calls "the solid upper middle" of his class. He had his subjects of lesser interest (math, chemistry) and those at which he excelled (English lit, world history, French), and through it all played centre on the basketball team and was into drama big time.

In his senior year, he did an International Baccalaureate course called "Theory of Knowledge," which he thrived on from beginning to end. It emphasized critical-thinking skills, to which I give a double thumbs-up, considering the extraordinary lack of them in the world these days.

'Do you really think you should be leading a tour of light-houses when you have a fear of heights?' he says to me a few days later. His new-found skills have their downside.

'We'll be walking up inside staircases, not scaling the outer walls.'

'Good point. Then again, that means a lot of stairs. Just don't look down.'

'I'll bear that in mind.' I smile indulgently.

'Assessing the risk factors, that's all.'

He is no doubt recalling the thirty–metre tumble I took down a rock embankment several years back in the course of leading a tour group. I survived admirably, despite the broken bones, but I would be the first to admit that it did make me somewhat wary of heights.

'I appreciate your concern.' Scoffing is unavoidable at this point.

He smiles, well aware that he's reached his limit. 'So,' he says, 'what's on the menu for tonight?'

His best friend, Kofi, is due to show up shortly and I prom-ised them dinner, although there's no sign I've made any moves in that direction.

'Takeout?' he speculates.

'Nope. Kofi is finally going to get his chance to show us what he's made of. I bought all the ingredients for jollof rice and chicken chichinga.'

'Chicken chichinga?'

'We've had it at the Farmers' Market. On a skewer, remember?' Kofi is originally from Ghana and his family has a food concession at the market on weekends. He helps his mother with the cooking, or so he says. This will be the test.

'Does Kofi know anything about this?'

'Nope.'

The doorbell rings. Dog Gaffer does his welcoming song and dance as Nick opens the door. 'Dad's got a surprise for you.' Kofi enters the kitchen, forewarned but not forearmed.

'Hey, Kofi, what's up, man?'

Like Nick, he's man-sized, both of them having levelled out close to my height, Nick a bit above (at six feet, to his immense satisfaction), Kofi a bit below.

'This is it, Mr. Synard. You know, free as a bird in the wind.' Kofi is known for readjusting idioms.

'Got a job for the summer?'

'Right-hand son in the kitchen.' Besides a spot in the market, his mother operates a catering business.

I'm smiling broadly. 'The man of the hour.'

Kofi is ready, willing, and, as it turns out, more than able. Within the hour, with the help of father-and-son sous-chefs, Kofi has set before each of us, seated at the kitchen table, a pair of skewers of chicken chichinga (pronounced in the proper Ghanaian way), each pair stretched temptingly beside a substantial mound of spicy tomato-red jollof rice.

'Looks fabulous, Kofi. You're the man.'

When it works its way past his modesty, the fellow has the most delightful smile. He and Nick have been fast friends since they started high school together. Sometimes I've suspected more than just friends, but I don't go there. Although they both have friends who are girls, neither has a girlfriend, in the traditional sense of the word. Which perhaps tells me something. I don't ask. Theirs is not the adolescence I grew up in. It has its own set of attitudes that I've yet to get my head around.

When all is said and done, they're a couple of pals now putting high school behind them and bound for university in the fall. Kofi is staying at home in St. John's and looks to be headed for a business degree at MUN. Nick, on the other hand, wants at least his first year away. He applied for the Foundation Year Program at the University of King's College in Halifax, with the encouragement of his high school English lit teacher. And was accepted. Too bad she hasn't offered to pay the tuition and residence fees.

The year at King's is what some people call the Great Books program: "An odyssey—a journey that takes you and your fellow travellers to thought-provoking, unfamiliar places, but one that ultimately brings you home." Who would say no to that? Not our Nick.

He's showed me the book list. Homer, Dante, Nietzsche, Chekhov, Virginia Woolf, and on and on. Lectures, tutorials, essay assignments. It seems to me a hefty workload. He figures, having conquered IB in high school, he's up for it. More power to him.

Actually, I'm envious. Nothing like that was even an option when I was going to university. Then, it was MUN or a trades school. I've never read Homer. Or Dante. So, yes, with his mother topping up an education fund we've been paying into since he was born, he's off to King's in the fall.

In the meantime, Nick's landed a job for the summer—waiter at one of the downtown restaurants. It starts at the end of June, when Water Street is turned into a pedestrian mall and each of the restaurants sets up an outdoor dining area. To his credit, he's determined to save most of what he makes as spending money for university.

Tough to think of him so grown-up that he's moving away from home. In the meanwhile, we'll make the most of our time together, which now is equal to the time he spends at his mother's place.

This is relatively new. Nick talked to Samantha about his living arrangement, so instead of spending more time with his mother, as he had since we divorced, they agreed he was old enough to decide the setup for himself. He wanted to even up the allocation. Two weeks with me, two weeks back with his mother. I think she saw it coming.

Occasionally it gets complicated—when one parent has to be away from home, or during school breaks. Nick, diplomat that he is, rearranges his scheduled days in such a way that his time with each of us evens out in the end. He's very good at avoiding parental sore points, and it's worked so far. Samantha and I are generally agreeable these days, exchanging smile for smile. We've come a long way, as Nick on one occasion pointed out, in what I took to be a slip of the tongue.

The *On the Rock(s)* tour I'm about to undertake has brought particular headaches. It falls squarely into our next two-week chunk of time together—further complicated because (surprise to me, as of yesterday) Samantha and her live-in, Frederick, have booked a getaway to Montreal for part of those two weeks.

Nick thinks it's just fine if he stays in my house by himself while I'm on the road chasing after lighthouses. 'Gaffer will keep me company. Nothing to worry about,' he says off-handedly. As if it's a foregone conclusion that he's old enough and mature enough to be left on his own, and that taking care of the dog somehow adds to the logic of it.

He's seventeen. I'm inclined to give him the benefit of the doubt, although not without reservations, given the stories I've heard about gangs of teenagers showing up uninvited at a house while the parents are away for a weekend, let alone a week or more. I have visions of my Scotch cabinet raided, empty bottles strewn about, upstairs and down.

His mother is even less keen on him staying alone. Needless to say, given that he's my responsibility for the two weeks, she's expecting me to come up with a solution that satisfies us both.

'The first part of the tour is not a problem, right?' says Nick, holding back from being argumentative. Sounding very level-headed. For a reason, I'm sure.

'Not a problem for the first three days. The lighthouses are day trips. Back home by suppertime. It's the week after that, when I'm crossing the island and heading into Labrador.'

'In that case . . .'

He hesitates, no doubt to be sure it comes out right. I can't wait.

'How about I come along, like Assistant Tour Guide?'

Well now. He's had his head wrapped around that for a while.

'Really?' I don't dismiss it out of hand, as I would have done even a year ago. He deserves an opportunity to build his case before I wreck it. I don't need an assistant. And what about Gaffer? He would hate being kennelled away from everyone he knows, which, in any case, would cost big bucks. Not in the cards.

'What size is the vehicle you're renting? How many passengers does it seat?'

'Seven.'

'Four doing the tour, plus you. Right?' That he knows already. 'In which case an empty seat for me, and another for Gaffer.'

'Ain't gonna happen. I can't spring this on the guests—cramped up with another person and a dog for a week.'

'They might all love dogs. Run it by them. See what they say.'

'Nick, man, this is not a solution.'

'Seems to me you have two choices. Either Gaffer and I stay here, or we go.'

Maybe there's a third. 'You could stay with Mae. She wouldn't mind.'

Mae is my significant other. We've been together for a while. She has her own place on Gower Street.

'Dad, really?'

He has a point. It would be totally awkward for him. And totally unnecessary, in his eyes.

'Besides which,' he says, 'isn't she meeting up with you at the end of the tour?'

That too. Mae is planning to fly across the island and connect with me after I finish up, for a little getaway of our own.

'By that time your mother will be back from Montreal. You'd only be staying with Mae for maybe five days.'

He's still far from keen on the proposition. This is getting all too complicated.

'I have another idea,' he says. Another deliberate pause. 'Think carefully before you say no.'

I can't wait, again.

'How about I take your car and drive in tandem with you across the island, me and Gaffer?'

I think carefully for about two seconds. 'Right.'

'No, I'm serious. It solves all the problems.'

'A waste of gas. You know how much gas costs these days. Plus you have limited experience with highway driving.' The kid got his licence no more than six months ago.

'Can't be any worse than driving the Outer Ring Road.'

It's the four-lane highway that circles St. John's, with multiple exits and speed demons who ignore road conditions. He's got a point.

'I'll be careful. You know me.'

He's got a second point. He's a very good driver. Aced his written test. Confident on the road without being cocky. At least when I'm in the car with him. Still, it's not an ideal solution.

But it is the only one either of us has come up with. As yet.

'Let's just leave it at that for now.'

I need breathing space. Time to myself with a drink of Scotch to weigh all the options. Time to argue it through with Samantha. There's got to be a way around this that satisfies us both.

We've three days to figure it out before the opening act of what I'm calling the *Right On! Light On!* tour gets under way. The subtitle was a sudden bit of inspiration to give a little flare, so to speak, to ten days on the road with four pharologists.

Three of the lighthouse addicts—Calvin Wright, Andy Fong, and Marco Tolentino—enjoy calling themselves pharologists. The fourth, André Bouchard, prefers *pharologue*. All are mainland Canadians, and each, in his own way, is a keener for the towering beacon. They've come to the right province.

Mentally, they might all be on the same track. But physically, they are all over the map. Calvin stands above the crowd, a lanky man whose clothes, although likely expensive when purchased, appear to have been hanging on the same frame for too long. He looks especially lean and elongated next to Andy, who maintains a lot of bulk for his limited height. On the other hand, the much younger Marco, although barely taller than Andy, is looking as if every inch of him has been gym toned. And as for André, he's kept in shape over the years that have now, like my own, begun to add up. I can already see I might pick up a few tips from him on dressing younger and looking cool.

The pharos four first met last year at Brock University during a symposium on eastern Canadian lighthouses that Calvin had organized. Although several Newfoundland and Labrador lighthouses had received considerable attention (no surprise there), few of those attending the conference had actually been to the province, including the gentlemen who are now set to join me in an attempt to atone for what Calvin referred to as "a major gap in our lighthouse life lists." (Kind of like birders, I was left thinking, only the subject is less elusive.)

Evidently, several others at the symposium had expressed interest in making the trek east, but in the end the number willing to commit had dropped to four. Last fall, out of the blue, I received an email from Calvin asking if such a tour was something I would be willing to arrange, and, if so, at what cost, and what I would propose as an itinerary? (The latter no doubt a test to see if I measured up to expectations.)

Such a tour opportunity doesn't come along every day. I researched intensely, came up with a budget and, although it wasn't stated outright, they were more than a little impressed. (I'd say it was the *Right On! Light On!* subtitle that clinched it.)

So here we are, six months later, at the starting gate. 'An eager eclipse of moths ready to be drawn to the light,' as I said to them when we met briefly last evening, after they had all checked into their hotel. No, they were not aware of the collective term for moths. Neither was I until a few hours before. As with any tour group I lead, participants need to be aware that an appreciation of the odd quip is essential if we are going to make the most of our time together.

We met over drinks in the hotel bar. I assumed they had all arrived in the province that afternoon, only to discover that two of them, André and Marco, had in fact come a few days earlier and taken a side trip together to Saint Pierre and Miquelon, French islands off the south coast of Newfoundland. I couldn't quite imagine it, given that they didn't appear, superficially at least, to have much in common. Of course, all four of them share a passion for lighthouses. Which, I get the feeling, is strong enough in these guys to overcome any disparities.

My objective for Day One of any tour is to make it a stunner. I want each participant to go to bed that first night thinking, 'Yes, this is all I ever hoped my odyssey with Sebastian Synard could be. And yes, it's going to be worth every last nickel I coughed up to be here.' I want each of them to lean over and blissfully turn out the bedside lamp, dying for daylight to come and the excitement to begin all over again.

I know it's a risk, but I start this Day One before daylight. I have them up and on the road by 4:30 for the drive to Cape Spear. Twenty-five minutes later, we're perched on bald rock next to the towering white ramrod of the present-day lighthouse. In the near distance is the cape's original one, the oldest lighthouse in the province still standing, now an interpretation centre.

The four position themselves, each a witness to sunrise at the easternmost point in North America. Calvin's focus is looking especially keen, with his greying professorial beard and moustache. (Rather too thick to my mind, as if compensating for his deeply receded hairline. I'm sure André would agree.)

Calvin is no doubt weighing the merits of my leadership so far. But yes, my friend, the rays of the beacon of all beacons strike you before they strike a single other person on the continent! And yes, here you all stand as the dawn breaks on . . . not one but two iconic lighthouses, famed in the annals of Newfoundland history.

Reluctantly, we make our way back to the city for breakfast. We return to this National Historic Site at ten, when the interpretation centre opens, for an in-depth look into the operation of a nineteenth-century lighthouse and the daily lives of the six generations of the Cantwell family who operated it. The day has definitely proven to be a stunner that leaves four hardened lighthouse-seekers reeling in the glow of a precisely planned, unforgettable opening act. *Right On! Light On!*

Day Two's centrepiece—nothing less than the lighthouse at Ferryland Head, an hour's drive south of the city, with an awesome secondary stop along the way.

As focused as the pharos four are on lighthouses (and let's be clear, lighthouses always take precedence), they had confirmed they were "somewhat" open to subsidiary activities, if such pursuits brought them within sight of rugged coastline. (Because, I could only assume, such terrain conjures up images of lighthouses.) The two-hour whale watching tour out of Bay Bulls to my mind fits the bill.

We've barely left the dock when Andy pipes up, 'Lots of whales off British Columbia. Including orcas and, of course, grey whales.'

Try not to be a downer, Andy.

'But no minkes,' I counter, as gently as I can. 'Or icebergs, or puffins. We're headed to a colony of half a million puffins, the largest in North America.'

'A very cute bird, I imagine.'

'An understatement, Andy.'

He sees just how darn cute. And how much more than cute is a massive iceberg. Or a pod of minke whales frolicking between it and the boat.

Andy and his buddies can't help but be impressed, even if "somewhat" against their will.

At their unequivocal direction, it is straight on then for Ferryland Head. We trek the final twenty minutes along a well-trodden, scenic trail from the parking lot until there it is—the red, iron-clad lighthouse, a fiery fixture for mariners since 1870.

I'm not about to break the spell, but Ferryland Head these days is less well-known for its lighthouse than it is for its Lighthouse Picnics. And here's the lowdown. Your consummate tour guide makes a reservation well in advance, having consulted participants on their menu preferences. We all show up at the building attached to the lighthouse and choose a blanket, plus a signal flag to designate our chosen grassy hillside perch. We sit and relish the spectacular vista that extends from the lighthouse behind us to the rugged coastline at our feet and then beyond to a far-off horizon not, thankfully, shrouded in fog today. Before we know it, our flag has been spotted and our gourmet lunches, together with Mason jars of freshly squeezed lemonade, arrive in a wicker basket.

'A+ for the food,' says Marco, well into his curried chicken sandwich. Marco is in his late twenties, I would guess. His parents emigrated from the Philippines, he has told us. Just from his tone of voice I sense he and his parents might not be on the best of terms.

'And A+ for atmosphere,' adds Calvin with a nod to the lighthouse. 'Not bad for automated.' Calvin is big on technology, less drawn to aesthetics. André, on the other hand, likes to stand at their bases and look up at length, analyzing the architectural line.

It goes without saying that they prefer their lighthouses manned, but there it is: you take what you can get, lads. The delectable picnic compensates hugely. As the well-fed Andy notes.

Of course, there are stories to be told. I defer to them for the site-specific lighthouse history. But as for the broader historical past, no one should set foot in Ferryland without realizing that in the early 1600s it was the site of one of the first English colonies in the New World, that George Calvert (a.k.a. Lord Baltimore) and his family left England and took up residence in a mansion house that once graced the shores of the small protected harbour, today the focus of an ongoing archaeological dig.

'And did you know that Lord Baltimore endured but one winter before abandoning Newfoundland and heading south to warmer climes?' They didn't. 'And did you know how the city of Baltimore got its name?' They didn't.

They turn to dessert. All too much peripheral information.

I smile indulgently. 'I'm sure Lord Baltimore would have built a lighthouse had he stayed.'

None of them thinks it's particularly funny. 'Not likely,' says Calvin. 'The oldest lighthouse in Britain wasn't built until 1669.'

'Not counting the Romans, of course,' inserts Andy, who, although he might not be as knowledgeable as Calvin, seems to enjoy adding small, pertinent detail. I sense a rivalry brewing.

'Oh, I'm counting the Romans, all right,' I counter.

Again, their humour is in short supply.

Yet on the drive back, they do, to a man, express their satisfaction at the day. They exit the vehicle more slowly than they climbed aboard this morning, always a good sign. My guess is they take a direct path to the hotel bar and intense lighthouse discussions beyond anything their tour guide would understand.

Day Three I call a double whammy. It'll take three hours to get to the lighthouse. But not a problem. The first whammy is just over halfway there.

As luck would have it, the lads are quick to fall asleep. Far too long at the bar, I suspect. Marco was looking particularly hungover at nine-fifteen. I hope he doesn't have a drinking problem. Been through that tour scenario before.

Forty minutes on the Trans-Canada brings us to the Salmonier Line. Literally a snoozefest all the way, which is just as well. Heading south and inland, we pass Salmonier Nature Park, a stop I had once considered but decided against. A good call, as it turns out. The lads would not appreciate a three-kilometre morning trek to lay eyes on a moose or struggle to find a pine marten hidden in the undergrowth. At this moment they are intent on prolonged sleep.

They begin to stir just as the coastline comes into view. I swear pharologists can smell salt water before they actually see it. I pull into one of the few spots left in the parking lot that faces St. Vincent's beach. Whammy number one.

The other vehicles are empty, their occupants having migrated to the stony shoreline, where they stand in clusters gazing seaward, cameras in excited hands. I sense an amazing tour moment about to unfold. The lads are in for a lot more than a whiff of salt sea air.

'I'm not seeing a lighthouse,' says Calvin.

No, Calvin, you are not. What you are seeing is nothing so static and inanimate.

'Neither do we,' says Andy, on behalf of the equally myopic threesome also looking about for a headland.

No, if you set your mind to it, what you would be seeing are living, breathing mammoths of the animal kingdom. 'Humpback whales feeding so close to shore that you can practically reach out and touch them. C'mon, we're missing out.'

The pharos four trail sluggishly behind me as I take off toward the shoreline. I don't bother to look back again. Eventually they catch up.

'Isn't this amazing?! The humpbacks are so darn close because the sea bottom drops right off there. Look at them breach!'

'Nature has its idiosyncrasies,' notes Calvin. The man works hard at sounding scholarly. He has a reputation to maintain.

Yes, you could say idiosyncrasies. If your brain were so out of sync with the natural world that it would take a whale to leap onto shore and flatten you before you'd appreciate its presence.

'It's like Marineland, except the whales don't do tricks.' That's Andy, sounding like God's gift to commercial theme parks.

Nor are they impressed with the life cycle of capelin, though I explain how in late June the small silver fish that have escaped the jaws of the whales roll up onshore to spawn. 'I've been on beaches where they've laid so many eggs it's like walking on sponge. Amazing.'

There are only so many times you can use the word "amazing" without a suitable response before you give it up as a lost cause. I turn and head back to the parking lot.

André catches up with me. 'No offence, Sebastian, but I've been in kayak in Saguenay Fjord and practically reached out and touched belugas. It was truly amazing.'

No point wrestling with such restricted minds. Let's get their collective eyes on a lighthouse, I'm thinking, before their indifference does permanent damage to my online ratings.

'Now you're talkin',' says Andy when, thirty minutes later, we're driving the gravel road at Portugal Cove South (directly past the turnoff to Mistaken Point, a UNESCO World Heritage Site, I will add), heading toward the immovable landmark of Cape Race. Still not automated, but also not animated.

I shouldn't be flippant. As lighthouses go, the all-white cylindrical shaft, twenty-nine metres of reinforced concrete, is quite striking.

André in particular is enthralled. '*Magnifique*,' he says. 'Spectacular.' André switches language with ease. I think he enjoys that it doubles his commentary.

The lighthouse is often the first landfall sighted by vessels crossing the Atlantic, destined for North America. In all its glory, and together with its foghorn, a resounding National Historic Site.

'Imagine it true to life,' declares André. 'Imagine it shrouded in fog. The catwalk and everything above it in the clouds, yet the light shining through.'

A metaphor for something, I'm sure. My intuition tells me André has a broad range of life experiences, most of which I don't expect to discover much about.

'April 14, 1912,' Calvin suddenly intones.

'CQD CQD SOS *Titanic* Position 41.44 N 50.24 W,' declares Andy, right on cue.

The others join in, like clockwork.

'Require immediate assistance.'

'Come at once.'

'We struck an iceberg.'

'Sinking.'

For those few moments, the pharos four reach a peak—they are an expertly oiled, incisively tuned chorus. Their hearts are pounding.

The distress message from the sinking *Titanic* was first received at the Marconi Station in Cape Race. As we all knew.

'At 10:25 p.m. EST,' I note, 'to be precise.' They glance at me with new, if momentary, respect.

To their minds, the wireless transmission is sacred text, or sacred Morse code. It gives the adjacent lighthouse a cachet that propels it to the very pinnacle of their Newfoundland lighthouse ranking.

That ranking is consolidated by the tower's "hyperradiant Fresnel lens." It seems that, as lighthouse lenses go, the one installed in the lantern room of the Cape Race Lighthouse is a supernova.

'The largest lens ever built,' Calvin is quick to point out. 'Only thirty-three ever installed, including at Cape Race in 1907. At the time the world's most powerful lighthouse, emitting one million candlepower.'

'Wow, that's a lot of wax.' My quip goes unnoticed.

'Less than ten in the world still in use,' Andy injects.

'Eight, to be exact,' responds Calvin. 'Not counting the partial biform in Bishop's Rock. Too bad they split the lens and put half of it in a museum.'

'Ah,' says Marco, anxious to contribute something. 'Bishop's

Rock, off Cornwall—such an icon. According to Guinness, the world's smallest island with a building on it.'

Which is something they all know, apparently, and the others deem unworthy of further comment.

Marco tries his best. He's not someone I would pick out of a crowd as a pharologist, given his fondness for wristbands and the silver ring piercing the upper edge of his ear. (Or the tattoos that I expect are lurking beneath the new black T-shirt he shows up in each day.) All the same, he's not particularly ill at ease among the other three.

As expected, the interior of the lighthouse is not open to the public. The lads stand well back from the base, binoculars at the ready.

'We have before us,' declares Calvin, gesturing upward and now in solid control, 'the sole working hyperradiant Fresnel lens in North America.'

I join them, sans binoculars, but looking suitably awestruck by this wonder of the lighthouse-lover's world.

It takes the rest of Day Three for Calvin, Andy, André, and, yes, Marco to come down from their unimaginable high.

LIGHT MY FIRE

'GAS TANK FULL?'

'Yes, Nicholas, it is, but we'll refrain from discussing what it cost, as anxious as you might be to do that.' Sarcasm at 7:45 on a Monday morning indicates a well-functioning brain. A solid start to the day.

It's Day Four and I'm scheduled to pick up the lads in fifteen minutes, from the Jag Hotel downtown. It's the start of our cross-island coastal romp, with Nick following dutifully behind. In my car, in tandem.

He's not saying much at this point. He knows it'll take a while before I have it sucked up completely.

Yes, all tanks are full. I built the stiff price of gas into the tour quote. The rental is a Dodge Durango SUV, hopefully with better fuel economy than I budgeted for.

Budgeted, of course, with a single vehicle in mind.

'All ready?' Nick says, Gaffer in his arms, waiting for the word before attaching the dog's harness to the restraint in the front passenger seat of my Toyota.

'As ready as we'll ever be.' Gaffer has already started to yelp. He's never been a fan of car travel.

Nick looks at me and attempts a smile. I detect an edge of restraint.

Restraint is good. We board our respective vehicles.

The Jag Hotel is notable for its '70s rock star vibe. The walls throughout the hotel are filled with framed photos of Jagger, Bowie, McCartney, et al. Our pharologists chose it for that very reason.

'If you can believe them, three of the four were happenin' dudes in their day. And as for Marco, his dude days are far from over.

After each of them had revealed an interest in these rockers, I had a brainwave. With Nick's input, I put together a playlist to brighten up, so to speak, the hours we'd have on the road. Each with "light" in the title. Inspired, or what? The only bummer—that iconic band Lighthouse didn't record such a song, at least not that I could find. "Sunny Days" came close, but not close enough.

"'Light My Fire,'" intones Nick, standing before the Doors in the lobby. The flame of Jim Morrison lives on.

'I'd say their lighthouse obsession was fuelled by a rebellious youth.'

"'Blinded by the Light,'" sings Nick, without missing a beat.

'Gotta be their theme song.'

Marco, the first of the pharos four, makes his appearance. Just as I'm about to introduce him to Nick, Andy and Calvin stroll in, and just behind them, André, making for a speedier collective intro. As luck would have it, Marco is from Markham, Andy is from Abbotsford, and Calvin is from St. Catharines.

André, however, is from Montreal. Handshakes and greetings all around, ending with '*Salut, ça va?*' from André.

'*Ça va bien,*' says Nick, which is a bit of a surprise to André, who's had little success speaking French to the boy's father.

André reverts to French whenever the opportunity comes his way. If the lighthouse falls under Parks Canada jurisdiction, there'll always be one attendant who's bilingual.

'Nick is coming along for the ride, so to speak. He and our dog Gaffer are following behind in our car. I hope you don't mind.' I had thought I might have been able to come up with a Plan B. No such luck. Let's leave it at that.

'I don't understand,' says André.

Okay. 'It works out better than if he stayed home alone. You know teenagers.'

Nick can barely control himself.

'No, what I don't understand is why he needs to drive,' says the dauntless André. 'You don't want to ride in our vehicle, Nick? *Il y a deux sièges vides.*'

Bypass the father, who got as far as the *Il y a deux*. My guess is two empty seats.

'Our dog is travelling with him,' I explain.

'What is he, an untrained pit bull?' says André, smiling broadly.

Nick returns the favour. 'Maltipoo,' he says, chuckling. 'Gaffer's a maltipoo.'

'My wife and I have a cockapoo,' says Andy.

It plays right into Nick's hands. It's a fine line he's walking, between his father and the two men edging into his camp.

'Less than twenty pounds,' adds Andy, 'and hypoallergenic.'

'Ditto,' says Nick, eyeing Andy and not me.

André looks at his fellow travellers. 'Who's good with Nick and Gaffer aboard our vehicle? Marco?'

'Fine with me,' says Marco. Ditto for Andy. Ditto for Calvin.

'Of course, it is up to you, Sebastian,' says André. 'Think of all you'll save with the price of gas these days.'

So, here we are, the Dodge Durango well past the city limits, all seats taken.

We're a congenial lot. Including Gaffer, who seems to have modified his distaste for confinement in a vehicle. The dog is upping his understanding of French, seated as he is between André and Nick, in the middle of the three back seats. I expect he'll be yelping with an accent before the trip is over.

'Look, Gaffer.' We're almost two hours out and approaching Goobies Junction. A favourite statue is about to make its appearance. 'Morris the Moose coming up!' Gaffer stands up and takes a gawk out the window.

My gear for the trip includes a small portable microphone and a speaker, positioned on the dash, which allow me to give an enriching running commentary on points of interest as we drive along, as well as make vital announcements. The microphone has proven to be well worth the investment. Strategic declarations, deft discourse—not just that, but the pharos four themselves take eagerly to the mic and each in turn spews untold amounts of knowledge about the lighthouse that is our focal point for the day.

'Time to see a man about a dog,' I announce, an expression inherited from my father.

Upon encountering Morris, Gaffer lifts a hind leg to the ungulate's hoof, while the rest of us take turns in the men's room of the tourist chalet nearby. Back outside, I find Marco standing head to flank with Morris.

'Moose are not native to Newfoundland,' I tell him. 'They were introduced in 1904. Today there's well over a hundred thousand.' As tour guide, I like to drop these historical nuggets whenever I can.

'I hunt moose in Northern Ontario,' responds Marco. 'I've downed three.'

'Are you serious?' Never would I have taken him for a big game hunter.

'Quite the rush,' he says, turning to walk back to the vehicle.

Nothing surpasses their Cape Race ranking. Despite the lineup of lighthouses we encounter on our trip across Newfoundland, the needle of the awe-o-meter does not edge past the 9.5 they awarded the *Titanic*/hyperradiant Fresnel combination.

It has escalated to a competition. At the end of each day, the lads total their individual marks, divide by four, and announce the group-designated score. A couple of lighthouses do come close to unseating the champ. Close but no cigar, as André is fond of saying. Each time, he brings forth the lighthouse-like shaft of a cigar tube, the Cuban contents of which he vows to smoke only after the score for the final lighthouse of the tour has been tabulated.

For the record, these are the scores of the lighthouses we visit on the cross-island segment of the *Right On! Light On!* tour.

Day Four: Cape Bonavista. Lighthouse keeper's residence has been restored to an 1870s look. We ascend the stone tower with costumed guide to get up close and personal with a "seal-oil fuelled catoptric light apparatus," of which there are very few to be seen anywhere in the world! Score: 9.25. (The sighting of puffins on cliffs nearby fails to impact the score.)

Day Five: Long Point, Twillingate. The lighthouse is perched atop Devil's Cove Head, not far from Horney Head Cove. Consider it the guiding light for Twillingate, the Iceberg Capital of the World. Its partly octagonal tower was encased in reinforced concrete after the original brick cracked due to an offshore earthquake in 1929! Score: 9.1. (Despite the stunning view through the lantern room's double row of triangular windows.)

Day Six: Rose Blanche, southwest corner of the island. The original light was the work of the Stevenson brothers of Edinburgh, father and uncle of Robert Louis Stevenson, author of *Treasure Island*! Its tower made up one end of the keeper's granite house, home in the 1920s to the keeper, his wife and sister, and fifteen children. A storm left the lighthouse in ruins . . . but more than fifty years later it was restored to its previous glory. Unique in all of Canada. Score: 9.15.

Day Seven: New Ferolle, partway up the Great Northern Peninsula. A stunner—the most stately of Newfoundland's lighthouses. A hexagonal concrete shaft of nineteen metres, each edge bearing a tapered buttress flaring out at the top to support the circular catwalk. A minimalist brilliant white expanse, capped by a red lantern room. Immortalized by one of Canada's most renowned painters, Newfoundlander Christopher Pratt. We stand back in wonder at its towering symmetry! We stand back and gaze at its all-consuming elegance! Score: 9.0. (Philistines, the pharos four, with the exception of André.)

WHEN THE LIGHTS GO OUT

AND HERE WE are, leaving New Ferolle behind, heading further up the Great Northern Peninsula and across the Strait of Belle Isle to Labrador. Late June: summer has finally arrived and our sights are set on the final lighthouse of the tour. It's the pièce de résistance. The highest lighthouse in the Atlantic provinces and the second highest in the whole of Canada. *Right On! Light On!* coming to its end in a blaze of glory.

The ferry docks in Blanc Sablon, Quebec. André is especially excited, even though it's only a few minutes to the provincial border with Labrador. He insists on stopping at the SAQ in Blanc Sablon for red wine, and then at an *épicerie* for a couple of baguettes, cheese, pâté, and smoked meat. What he really needs is the opportunity to let loose with full-on, uninhibited conversation with his fellow Québécois.

When he emerges from the *épicerie* (his buddy Nick behind him, carrying another bottle of wine), he's revved up and ready to take on whatever else the evening has to offer. That would include takeout from Fast Freddy's in L'Anse-au-Loup.

So: baguettes, etc., plus chicken and fries around the firepit of the Grenfell Louie A. Hall B & B in Forteau, before we tackle the lighthouse in the morning. We're a congenial but reflective lot, a tad sad at the realization that after tomorrow we'll no longer be the pharos four + two + dog. The mainlanders will be flying out of Deer Lake and back to where lighthouses are forced to take second place to the mundane details of their everyday lives. It's inevitable, but the Fresnel lenses must grow dim.

Surprisingly, it is Marco who takes a stab at summing up their tour experience.

'We landed high on lighthouses. We fly away pumped because we got off on them even more.'

Sounds like he's had it stored in his brain for a while, ready for release at the appropriate time.

None of the other three respond. A bit of a strain, I'm sure, but nonetheless good on them for giving Marco his moment.

Their attention turns to making the most of the remainder of the tour. The wine flows freely, including into the glass gripped by Nick's adolescent hand. I'm well aware the French have a laissez-faire take on teenagers and wine. Given that Nick and André have knocked together a solid friendship over the past few days, I take it as only expected they should share what I note to be an exceptional Cahors that would never find its way into our Newfoundland liquor outlets.

André knows his wines and he relishes the opportunity to educate the young fellow's inexperienced palate.

'Let it linger, play about your taste buds,' he tells Nick. 'Revel in the earthiness before you swallow.'

Which is very similar to what Nick has overheard me tell friends of mine when we're sampling a new Scotch. What can I say but, 'Great wine, André.'

'Yeah, great wine, André,' echoes Nick, smiling broadly at me.

I retrieve one of the two bottles of Scotch I've brought

along on the trip and from which I've been drawing a dram at the end of each day. As with what remains of André's wine, it's a rather pleasant way to continue the fete around the firepit.

Only Calvin and André have much interest in Scotch. I pour a dram of the Laphroaig Quarter Cask for each of us. Marco and Andy prefer the beer they purchased when we stopped for gas on our way up the peninsula. To each his own. Good to see it's a local craft beer and not the Budweiser that passed their lips earlier in the week. Nick makes the most of the wine left in his glass.

I up everyone's drinking experiences with a plate bearing small bars of fine, single-origin, Newfoundland-made chocolate. A little extra something to bring forth as the tour is winding down, to further embed the memory of the singular charm of the past week.

The plate makes the rounds.

'Don't chew the chocolate,' Nick announces, just as I'm about to. 'Let it melt in your mouth. Just like Scotch, let it linger on your taste buds. Swallow only when you have to.' Outmanoeuvring me. Revenge of a sort. He catches my eye and winks, the lovable smartass.

By Labrador standards, it's a warm evening. A little wind to keep the flies at bay, which is always a bonus. We're all good, all mellow. Including Gaffer, who is curled at Nick's feet, near the fire.

Even Calvin, who up to this point seemed to be in permanent cerebral mode, has let down his hair a little, despite what's on his head being in short supply.

'This reminds me of the time I spent in Scandinavia, except we'd be drinking aquavit.'

'And when was that, Calvin?' asks André, as interested as we all are in discovering another side of the man.

'In my twenties. I was just getting into lighthouses. Drinking aquavit in the bar of the coastal ferry. Some very memorable nights.'

'I'd say you were into more than lighthouses,' injects Marco.

'What was her name?' prods André.

Calvin waits out the laughter. 'Let's just say I acquired a taste for aquavit.'

That's as far as he's willing to take it.

'You be very happy to know, Calvin, that there's an aquavit made right here in the province. By the Newfoundland Distillery Company.'

'Unbelievable. In which case I expect I'll be taking a bottle back home with me.'

There follows a downtime in the conversation. A good point at which to inject a little historical background about the B & B that I've chosen for the last two nights of the tour. Normally it would have come from the owner, but yesterday I received an email from her with a list of room assignments and a note that she wouldn't be able to meet us when we arrived. 'The front door will be unlocked. Make yourselves at home,' she had written. She would see us later in the evening.

The lads had noticed right away that the Grenfell B & B was not your ordinary guesthouse. Why the names above the bedroom doorways—Jean Skelly Room, Mary Fowler Room, etc.? Why the displays of artifacts in the hallway and sitting room, a lot of them medical instruments? Why the framed black-and-white pictures from the 1930s?

'I'm in the Nursing Aid Room. Weird, very weird,' says Andy. 'Just the thought of blood freaks me out.'

Overly squeamish, Andy? Who said anything about blood?

'What we're sleeping in, gentlemen, is a former Nursing Station—'

'I suspected as much,' declares Calvin.

'—one of several built along the coast of southern Labrador and northern Newfoundland through the fundraising efforts of Sir Wilfred Grenfell.'

'Never heard of the man.' Andy again. But he's not the only one.

'Dr. Grenfell was a medical missionary from England,' pipes up Nick. 'Back in the day, he brought medical care to thousands of people along this coast who never had it.' Nick knows this because he once did a heritage fair project on Sir Wilfred.

This encourages a father-son synopsis of the remarkable man who helped reshape the living conditions of this remote, forgotten part of the world. The lads have come to expect me to run off at the mouth about local history, but not teenage Nick. They are impressed as much by his enthusiasm as by his narrative. It does a father's (and ex-history teacher's) heart a great deal of good.

'Pour him a dram,' says André. 'He's earned it.'

Now then. What do I say to that?

'I'm not big on Scotch,' Nick tells him. 'Am I, Dad?' As if I might have offered it to him at some point in the past. Which I never have. I realize he's letting me off the hook.

'I figure I'll grow into it,' he says.

At that moment, a pair of vehicles can be heard making their way along the gravel road leading to the B & B. Gaffer emits a mildly disapproving bark. The vehicles park side by side. Their drivers' doors open, two women get out, the headlights fade away.

The first, exiting a hefty pickup, must be the owner of the B & B. From the other vehicle, a sporty green Mini Cooper, a tall, slim, younger woman has emerged. Wearing shorts and hiking boots, shouldering a backpack and toting what looks to be a camera bag. Close-cut, stylish brown hair. I'm thinking midtwenties.

'Peggy,' I say, hand outstretched, advancing to meet the seemingly energetic, congenial owner. 'We did as you suggested. Made ourselves right at home.'

In the course of being introduced to the rest of our group, Peggy Hancock not only confirms all I've said but is excited to add that both she and her spouse Dwight were born in the former Nursing Station that they now operate as a B & B.

The pharos four don't quite know how to respond. Childbirth is not among their repertoire of conversation topics.

'I avoided assigning any of you gentlemen the Ladies' Ward, where my mother gave birth to me.'

Andy winces. 'Let's not get into that.'

A put-on, it seems to me.

Peggy smiles his way. 'Wouldn't want you to have nightmares about wailing youngsters. You're on holiday after all.' Her smile is returned, if stiffly. 'That particular room I put aside for Amanda.'

That would be Amanda Thomsen, who raises a tentative hand to everyone as Peggy adds, 'Amanda is in the area to spend time at some of our historic sites, including the Point Amour lighthouse, as part of a project she's working on.'

The lads perk up. Suddenly a topic of conversation they can very much relate to, and with an attractive young woman at that.

'You're welcome to join us after you settle in,' I tell her. 'We're all what you might call lighthouse enthusiasts.'

'Absolutely. We'd love to hear about your project,' adds Marco, with a little too much enthusiasm. Then again, he's the only one of the four anywhere near her age.

She makes no promises, but a half-hour later, after Peggy has gone back home for the night, Amanda reappears and seats herself in the additional Adirondack chair that the especially hopeful Marco has set near the fire, next to his.

She sits upright rather than easing herself against the back of the chair. She's trying to look relaxed, but doesn't quite bring it off, which is understandable given we're six males, all strangers.

'Would you like a cold beer?' Marco asks. He offers three choices from his stash of RagnaRöck, which has become his craft brew of choice.

'Or Scotch?' I offer. I've noticed a definite increase in the number of young women showing up at WhiskyFest in recent years.

She opts for an IPA. 'I know this brewery,' she says. 'It's in St. Anthony, where our project is based.' She's found a lead in to conversation.

Amanda, as it turns out, is from St. John's. She, together with two others (a photographer and the project manager) are working with the regional tourist development association to research, illustrate, and write what will be a coffee-table book showcasing the distinctive attractions of the area. Of which there are many, lighthouses not the least among them.

Marco exits to the kitchen, returning in record time with a glass and an open can. 'Freyja's session IPA,' he says as he pours it for her. 'I'm into Odin's cream ale myself.'

Really, Marco, that's good to know. I hadn't noticed it before, but the brewery has a Viking vibe. I see it now on the label.

'This will be my third lighthouse,' Amanda continues. The lads are all ears. They're wanting to know the others, or what might be on her to-do list. No doubt contemplating what they're missing by focusing on only one lighthouse for our last day. I remind them they had agreed that, given our time constraints, Point Amour was the obvious choice.

'Quirpon Island was special.'

I had hoped she wouldn't mention it. It had been the subject of an exhaustive debate during the back-and-forth planning for the tour. A lighthouse on a small island off the northern tip of Newfoundland. Accessible only by boat, with the only other structure on the island a B & B opened by an entrepreneurial couple wanting to give those willing to make the effort to get there "the exclusive experience of a lifetime." In the end, it was clear we couldn't fit it in.

No need to flog a dead horse, gentlemen. 'In any case, light-house for lighthouse, it could never match Point Amour.'

'That's true,' Amanda says, glancing at me and sensing she had struck something of a sore point.

Gaffer's senses are equally well tuned. He, too, has come to the conclusion that I could use a little help. He's been eyeing Amanda since she arrived, especially once she made the effort to pet him. He skirts her chair, then unceremoniously jumps up and curls himself into her lap. Just what was needed to end the lighthouse talk. She turns all her attention to the dog.

I apologize for Gaffer's unexpected leap, but there's no need. I can see he is also helping her keep Marco at bay.

I discourage Nick from going in search of more wood for the fire, allowing it instead to burn to embers and die a natural death. Tomorrow *Right On! Light On!* reaches new heights. We want everyone well rested and at the top of their game.

'See you at breakfast, folks.' I add a chipper 'Good night.' Nick gathers a reluctant Gaffer and follows me to the B & B's front steps.

'Gaffer needs a walk,' I tell him. A well-voided dog always ups the chances of a good night's sleep.

Nick attaches the dog's leash and checks his pockets to be sure he has the requisite bag. He doesn't mind being the one to do it, given how good he is at walking while simultaneously texting his friends back in St. John's.

As the pair walk off, Amanda arrives. I suspect she's used

our exit as a prompt to make her escape. We enter the B & B together.

'They can be a bit annoying sometimes. But they're a good lot generally.'

'You mean Marco? Don't worry. I have a black belt in interpersonal relationships.'

I suspect she's being funny, but I'm not entirely sure. Regardless, she's made a point.

'In that case, would you care to join us for dinner tomorrow evening? We have a reservation at the Florian.'

She hesitates. 'That's very kind of you.'

'The reservation is for six-thirty. Works for you?'

'Yes.' We exchange cell numbers in case there's a change of plans.

'Good night,' she says. 'I'll see you at breakfast.'

There was a time (not so long ago, not that I care to remember) when I might have been the one requiring Amanda to don her black belt. There was a post-divorce sequence of one-nighters, most of which left me, once the hangover subsided, feeling dumb-ass sorry for myself.

That scenario, I'm more than happy to report, has changed. I have one person to thank for that.

'Hi, how are you?' I'm asking her within five minutes. 'Not long now.' I've taken one of the couches in the empty sitting room.

'I'm good. Busy day at the shop. I'm really looking forward to the break.' Mae is due to fly into Deer Lake on Sunday, shortly after the tour ends and the pharos four fly off, connecting to the various places in Canada that have agreed to welcome them back.

'I can't wait. A chance to kick back and relax. And, as far as is humanly possible, put lighthouses out of my mind.'

She chuckles. 'Anything you need? Scotch?'

'That too.'

I suddenly catch the sound of someone opening the front door. And closing it again. Whoever it is, he's trying to be as quiet as he can.

He has less luck ascending the stairs. They creak with each step.

'I'd better go.' Which Mae knows by now is code for the tour needing my attention. 'Love you. I'll be in touch tomorrow.' I pocket the phone and ease my way along the hallway to the bottom of the stairs, by which time whoever was walking up them has reached the top and disappeared.

I stand and listen. Not that it should be any of my business. Curiosity more than anything.

There's a quiet knock on a door. And a short while later, a second. Then a third.

In what I take to be about thirty seconds, a door opens. And eventually closes again. I return to the sitting room and check through a window to see who's still around the firepit.

I have one conclusion—that it was Marco who went up the stairs. With two possible results—her door opened and closed. Or his did.

PRAISE THE LORD,
I SAW THE LIGHT

ONE OF THE joys of a B & B is, of course, waking up to a home-cooked breakfast. Since my happy encounter with the intermittent fasting regime a few years back, with which I shed twenty pounds, breakfast regularly turned to brunch and usually didn't start until at least eleven o'clock. Black coffee on its own was the order of the morning.

It would, however, be sinful to hold to such a habit in light of the array of breakfast options Peggy has set out on the dining room table. I am the first to show up, having already walked and fed Gaffer and secured him to the deck outside. Nick will eventually, at his own sluggish morning speed, find his way to the table.

A still-warm selection of cinnamon rolls, scones, and muffins vie for consumption with a parade of homemade jams in Mason jars—partridgeberry, blueberry, blackberry, and every other berry that grows wild under the Labrador sun, including the much-prized bakeapple (alias cloudberry).

I'm still pondering the choice as Amanda slips into the

dining room, looking pleased to find only one other person at the table.

'Good morning,' I say. It appears she enjoyed a sustained night of rest. 'Beautiful outside. Sunny and getting warmer.'

'Perfect.' She takes a seat at the end of the table, then repositions some cutlery and sets down her camera.

'The lighthouse will be in its glory. And the pharologists will be in theirs.'

Only now does she look directly at me. 'Do you know what Carl Jung said about light?'

What was that? I'm mid-scone and ill-prepared. As I chew, I'm thinking she means the Carl Jung of first-year university, Psychology 101, which I barely passed.

'He said, "The sole purpose of human existence is to kindle a light in the darkness of mere being."'

Really. 'I'm not surprised,' I lie. I'm just lost for an intelligent response.

She looks away. 'A phallic symbol, really.'

Make that lost twice over. A bite of scone kills several seconds. A drink of coffee a few more.

A humorous taunt to start the day? A little innocent mischief? She's definitely unbound by the conventions of breakfast conversation.

She's smiling to herself. 'At that height, no worries about getting it up, up, up.'

This is going nowhere promising. 'Have a scone, Amanda. They're delicious.'

She's more interested in her camera. She lifts it up and, pushing back her chair, appears to begin scrolling through images on its monitor. She stops at one.

'Fuck.' She continues scrolling without looking up. 'What about you, Sebastian, are you game to go all the way . . . in a lighthouse? You must like to come out on top.'

I don't quite get it—her manner or the character switch. Or know how I should react. For whatever reason she's pushing the boundaries.

'We all have our ups and downs,' she says, 'some harder than others.'

She must be upset about something. Covering it up by being provocative. Something to do with Marco maybe.

'I'm old enough to be your father.'

She has no response.

'Like I tell Nick when he has a rough day: *Behind the clouds, the sky is always blue.*' I don't know where I first heard it, but for some reason it stuck with me. A bit maudlin, but it serves its purpose.

She's lifted her head. It seems as if she might say something, but at that moment the first of the pharos four makes his appearance.

'Hey, Amanda,' Andy says. 'What's up?'

She takes a moment. 'Planning my day.'

He pours himself a coffee. Bit heavy on the sugar there, Andy. You're in for a long climb today. Yes, why not two scones while you have the chance, as long as there's room on the plate for those three spoonfuls of jam.

He does hesitate on a fourth. 'Bakeapple. Never heard of it.' An obstacle easily overcome.

The fourth spoonful takes its place even before Amanda notes, 'The rarest of Labrador berries. Not to everyone's taste. But I'm sure you'll love it.'

As I have observed during the week, Andy's is not a discriminating palate. He likes to have a go at it all. The muffin and cinnamon roll are waiting dutifully in line.

André and Calvin are next to appear. They acknowledge us earlier birds and go straight for the coffee. For André it's a quick pivot and out the front door for a cigarette. Gaffer will appreciate the company.

'Here we are,' says Calvin. 'All ready for the climax of the tour.'

I'm curious to see just what Amanda will do with that.

She sits in silence, her camera set aside, attentive to a yoghurt cup she's retrieved from the small stockpile in the centre of the table.

Nick finally makes his appearance, still getting himself up to speed. He pours a glass of orange juice and selects a muffin. 'André and Gaffer are outside.' He exits to join them, relieved to escape anyone's expectation of him being alert.

And now for the person we've been waiting for. Marco strolls in.

I'm expecting sheepish. What I get is smug.

'I hope everyone is feeling half as good as I am.'

Well then, Marco. Life dealt you a particularly promising hand this morning? Even though you're not actually showing it.

'The cinnamon rolls are very tasty,' Amanda says, without looking at him. She hasn't eaten one. 'I assume you slept well?' She pours herself a cup of coffee. They've yet to make eye contact.

'I assume we all did,' he says blandly.

I assume nothing except there's a distance between them.

André and Nick re-enter and fill the remaining spots at the table. A change for the better. We are, by all outward appearances, an amiable crowd, united in focus, bonded by the prospect of what awaits us at Point Amour.

'Well, men, this is the big one. Erected to a height out-stripping all the others.' She takes a look around the table. 'It's what your dreams are made of. You must be excited.'

Just when I thought she had mellowed.

'We're excited all right,' Andy says, Amanda's allusion making a direct pass over his head. 'It's the full meal deal.'

Amanda retrieves her camera, pushes back her chair, and stands up. 'See you all at supper. Enjoy your time at the light-house. Hey guys, what's the difference between light and hard?'

Off she goes then, finally.

There's a prolonged pause.

'Okay, so what *is* the difference?' A succession of shrugs.

Except for Nick. The kid is looking sheepish. We wait him out.

'You can sleep with a light on.'

It's Day Eight. As some would have it, the climax. I prefer culmination—the culmination of a well-orchestrated expedi-tion, bringing us to the site of the premier light station along this rugged coast, this bulwark against the North Atlantic.

Yes, as we ride the Durango over the fifteen kilometres from Forteau's historic B & B to Point Amour's storied monolith, lighthouse playlist turned up an extra notch, there is a decidedly positive atmosphere pervading the group. Not only in antici-pation of the next several hours, but in acclamation of the several days just past. Life for four inquisitive pharologists has been very good.

The honour of mic commentary has fallen to Marco. The least seasoned of the four, he looks as if he's feeling a certain pressure to perform well.

'It took three years to build and was completed in 1857. It was built of limestone quarried in Forteau Point and L'Anse-au-Loup. The foundation is on bedrock. The base walls are six feet thick.' Et cetera.

Not much life in the lad. The others are waiting for some anecdote to liven up the narrative. There must be plenty, considering the age and size of the beast.

But Marco is just not in the storytelling mood. Melancholic residue from what did or did not take place with the enigmatic

Amanda? Whatever the case, as his narrative is about to die a
natural death, I step in to offer a much-needed boost.

'How interesting, Marco. Thanks. It leads me of course to
the question of the origin of the name Point Amour. And of
L'Anse Amour, the small community adjacent to it.'

'Shouldn't it be *Pointe* Amour?' calls André from the
back. 'Like *Pointe*-au-Père Lighthouse? Which is also a National
Historic Site, by the way.'

Quebec lighthouses are André's forte. Which we are reminded of regularly.

'Great question, *mon ami*.'

'*Bien sûr*.' André always relishes a little language jousting.

'*Messieurs*, my research would indicate that its original name
may well have been *Pointe aux Morts*.' To offset the vacant stares
from the other three pharos, I add, 'As in Dead Man's Point.'

'As in *L'Anse aux Morts*?' prods André. 'As in Dead's Man's
Cove.'

He's right. 'All those shipwrecks before the lighthouse was
built.'

'You mean,' says André, 'the English built the lighthouse and,
in a bout of optimism, changed the name to Point Amour?'

'*Aux Morts*, Amour,' pipes up Nick. 'I like the harmony
of the irony.' Hand it to the lad for upping the level of discourse. Yes, he'll give King's College a good run for its money
this fall.

The other three pharologists have had more than enough
of this translation talk. Fortunately, the dwellings of L'Anse
Amour/*L'Anse aux Morts* are making themselves known in the
distance, just beyond which will be our pole star.

In the meantime, let's make a brief stop at the "Oldest
Funeral Monument in North America," shall we? The gents are
none too pleased, but in this case I'm not about to give them a
choice. A prehistoric marvel overrides their single-mindedness.

Along this road is a mound of boulders, a site excavated by archaeologists in the 1970s and found to hold the skeleton of a child and a cache of grave goods carbon-dated to 7,500 years ago. Stunningly significant. Far more so, in fact, than the lighthouse at the end of the road (although, perish the thought, I'm not about to suggest that to the pharos four).

It's enough to lure them out of the vehicle and onto the viewing platform, peering past the railing to the circular mound of lichen-covered boulders. The burial mound holds them for all of thirty seconds.

'*Intéressant*,' says André.

Really, André, that's all you can come up with? Your urban mindset is showing through.

Calvin, equally inconversant with the pre-pharos universe, takes the comment as a cue to lead the way back to the Durango. 'We're good to go,' he says shamelessly.

I take my own darn time, thank you. I'm smugly thrilled to discover that we have to drive past the village, around a prominent escarpment, along a nondescript four kilometres of dirt road, all before even catching sight of a lighthouse.

But, in the end, there it is—the thirty-three-metre white cigar tube with a single black stripe, its catwalk and lantern room topped by a red cupola.

The lads fidget. When I bring the Durango to a slow halt on the parking lot, they are already out of their seats and rabid for an unencumbered view of their lightship.

It's unnerving really, the collective excitement aimed at this inanimate object.

Pause . . . okay, I'm being unfair. Not to mention hypocritical. After all, I'm the one who ferried them here. And raided their wallets in doing so. I should put a lid on it and join in the revelry.

'Well, lads, this is it, the one we've all been waiting for. The pinnacle. The peak. The zenith. Damn it all, the Holy Grail.'

'The dazzling cosmic light at the end of the tunnel,' murmurs Andy, as if we've set stakes down on sacred ground.

The other three are equally awestruck. Their cameras hang unheeded against their chests. I seize the moment for the deepest appreciation of what they truly are—unabashed, unrepentant pharologists.

And for that moment, I relish the fact that I am the one responsible for this encounter, one that will be forever ingrained in their memories of their time on planet Earth.

Gaffer barks. The spell dissipates. The dog has always been good at injecting reality when necessary. He needs his walk.

'The lighthouse is uplifting to say the least,' quips Nick. His humour is underappreciated. He looks at me, surprised he's misread the crowd.

Nevertheless, they need to vacate nirvana and actually enter the building. In the meantime, Nick will take Gaffer for his morning jaunt, before confining him to the Durango and joining us inside.

'Okay gentlemen, deep breaths. Set yourselves in motion to extract every last ounce of this pharological experience.'

They're impressed with my use of "pharological," while I'm not sure it's even a word. Nonetheless, it sets them in a near radiant frame of mind, ready to enter the lighthouse.

As they all know, attached to it are the former living quarters of the lighthouse keeper, his assistant, and their families. It's now an interpretation centre, with much of it restored to its nineteenth-century character. The lads cross the threshold ahead of me and step purposefully inside. I quickly take care of the entrance fees.

The interior has an abundance of illustrated storyboards sharing space with antique furniture and artifacts. They're keen on it all, upstairs and down. Their aim is to supersize the info they've amassed from the internet.

'I didn't know that,' says Andy, his voice coming from the floor above. Even though there's a lot he does know, such words are music to a tour guide's ears. Yes, Andy, there's a lot to learn.

Especially about international maritime signal flags. Who knew?

Upstairs in an ancient wooden chest, each flag lies coiled comfortably in its own slot. The lads find unexpected rewards in the hands-on experience of randomly choosing one and unfurling it. They display different combinations of yellow, white, blue, red and black in squares, stripes and triangles, the colours and patterns chosen for their visual impact from a distance.

'The real thing,' says André, meaning not New Age nylon. 'Beautiful craftsmanship.' Transported back decades by the touch of thick, weathered cotton. Sweet.

They look closer at the chest's open lid and find secrets of the lighthouse's history lying naked before them. The interior of the lid is covered with signatures and messages pencil-scratched into the wood, an invitation to kneel and eyeball them intently, in an attempt to decipher the now-faded handwriting.

Without much success.

But they have another plan. Calvin, who sports a Samsung Galaxy (whose picture quality, he would have us believe, outsmarts that of any other smartphone on the market), systematically records every square centimetre of the surface. When he returns home, he will assemble the segments into a composite. And the lads will spend a good part of the forthcoming Canadian winter deciphering and, when that doesn't work, speculating on what has been written on the chest lid over the life of the lighthouse. I smell a forthcoming article in *Lighthouse Digest*.

The foursome is back to being utterly pumped, and we have yet to enter the lighthouse tower. Still ahead—the apotheosis of the past eight days, the cosmic cluster at the end of a dark, vertical tunnel.

Nick is as turbocharged as any of them. He has whipped through the interpretation centre and stands, shuffling his feet restlessly, near the first of the steps leading to the top of the tower. Got to love it. Got to think: as a father, you've done something right when you see your teenage son get this excited about setting eyes on a second-order Fresnel lens.

Visitors can only climb the tower stairs with one of the lighthouse staff leading the way. The older, experienced Marsha, in charge of the site it would appear, has had a fix on us since we first arrived. She knows keeners when she sees them. And, I assume, she's looking forward to making use of the full range of her knowledge about the lighthouse, rather than having to answer humdrum, run-of-the-mill questions.

'Well, folks,' she says when she joins us, 'all systems go? We're talking 132 steps up a tower that has a diameter of 24 feet here at ground level, narrowing to 8 feet at the top. Generally winding staircases with landings, but the last dozen steps are a straight-up ladder. Are you up for it? Claustrophobia, anyone? Acrophobia? Vertigo?'

How about just plain out of shape? I glance at Andy. Is he about to admit to anything? Not on your life.

Nick glances at me. Am I about to admit to a slight case of acrophobia? (Very slight, I will add.)

I speak for everyone when I tell Marsha, 'We're good to go.'

And so the ascent begins. A slow climb to the candescent carrot at the end of a rather steep stick.

My wits are under firm control. In any case, the first fifty stairs are a cinch. Generously wide spiral, beautiful landings, the occasional window cut through stone walls six feet thick. All immaculate, except for the occasional indifferent spider. (Marsha forgot arachnophobia.)

'All good?' says Nick, looking over his shoulder. He's one step ahead of me and two behind Andy, the last in line of the pharos four.

As reluctant as I am to respond to Nick's less-than-subtle probe, I give in, with a smile, overly broad. 'Jim-dandy.' He likes it when I use outdated idioms. He chuckles. It also puts him off his game.

'Everyone okay?' Marsha calls down the stairwell from her position as leader of the pack. I sense she is seeing a gap between the lads and wondering why everyone is not managing to keep up, given the relaxed pace she has set.

The answer would be Andy. A man in denial if there ever was one. Let's not go there, however. Let's play along and try to keep the congeniality intact.

Still, the rear end trio remains in a slump. Andy's comrades up ahead can smell the second-order Fresnel, yet Marsha is unwilling to have them press on and leave Andy in their wake. She fears cardiac arrest.

Having spent a week with the man, I feel confident that there's nothing to worry about. He has given in to the pace that works for him, such as it is. Not that his companions have shown any increase in sympathy over time. As demonstrated by Marco.

'Get the lead out, Andy, man.'

The diameter of the tower has continued to narrow, along with the width of the spiral staircase and its steps. As expected. We've come a long way. A hundred and twenty steps, to be exact. I've been counting.

In Andy's own good time, we reach the landing at the base of the ladder that will deliver us to the lantern room and bring us face to face with the revered lens. At the landing are waiting Marsha and the impatient three.

I've gone ninety per cent of the way to the top, with only

minor queasiness. I feel reinvigorated. Ready to reinsert myself as the tour guide who has set these lads exactly where they are at this moment.

'Well, gentlemen, here we are, about to score the big one, the jewel in the crown.'

'Yes, *messieurs*,' inserts André, 'and look who put that jewel in place.'

His hand is pointing to the words cast into what looks to be an iron support column for the lantern room above our heads. They read L. SAUTTER & C$^{\underline{IE}}$ CONSTRUCTEURS, A PARIS. The whole column painted a bright red.

'Louis Sautter and Company, manufacturer of the Fresnel lens,' says André. For my benefit and Nick's, since the other three would never have the audacity to call themselves pharologists if they didn't already know that tidy bit of information.

'And what would this be, André?' Let's see just much louder he can blow his own horn. I'm pointing to a rectangular metal frame, painted the same bright red, outlining an opening through the stone wall. An iron rod attached to the frame secures a wooden hatch that covers the exterior end of the opening. Antiquated, but it has probably been doing the job for a hundred years.

'The access, *bien sûr*, to the catwalk.'

'*Bien sûr*,' chimes Nick. 'What were you thinking it was, Dad?'

Bien sûr. Bien sûr. Of course it's the access to the catwalk. It's not like I wasn't about to figure that out.

Let's move along, shall we.

'Marsha, I'm assuming it's off limits?'

'To all but the window cleaners. Or with special permission.'

'What exactly does it take to get special permission?' asks Marco. Always one to test the boundaries.

'I'm afraid you have to go through the Labrador Straits

Historical Development Corporation. It administers this site.'

'Not necessarily a lengthy process?' says Marco. Pharologists live in hope.

'You would need good reason. It's not open to tourists, I'm afraid.'

Marco considers himself much more than a mere tourist. His boundless interest in lighthouses would be more than good reason. Nevertheless, he's smart enough to know that bureaucracy doesn't have a fast track. He looks tempted but doesn't pursue the matter.

I rub my hands together in an attention-grabbing display of eagerness. 'Lead the way, Marsha. We're incredibly excited about the lantern room!'

A ladder is not my favourite means of ascent, but this one is flanked by handrails and is riveted in place top and bottom. It's solid iron. It's not going anywhere. The others have forged ahead, behind Marsha. I take the first step, bringing up the rear with confidence.

It suddenly occurs to me that any danger is not in the ladder itself but in the form of Andy struggling up the steps ahead of me. Were he to collapse, it would be like a 250-pound sack of concrete plummeting into me, sending both of us crashing to the iron landing below. Good God, get that out of your head, Sebastian. That's not how you want to die.

Andy makes it to the top and, with a hand from Nick, lands upright on the lantern-room floor. I am also not above accepting a helping hand. With control of my breathing comes a new lease on life.

Other than Nick, nobody is paying any attention to me. All pharologist eyes are on the formidable Fresnel. Fully recovered, I, too, stand in awe of this marvel of lighthouse lenses, its hundreds of polished glass prisms set into precise configuration. A jewelled beehive. A work of art.

Marsha has her commentary well rehearsed, lines she uses no matter the knowledge base of her audience. 'The light was first lit in 1858 by five large concentric wick lamps burning whale oil. Over time, the lighting source changed to lanterns that used kerosene, then petroleum vapour, to the electric apparatus we have today. Through it all, this Fresnel lens remained in place.'

While she's taking a breath, Calvin launches himself into the lead, as if Marsha's words had been merely a cue for someone to expand on what she has to offer. She's surprised, but open to audience participation.

Calvin, too, is well rehearsed. In fact, he could just as well be taking the stage as keynote speaker at a symposium on lighthouse lens technology. 'What you have before you is, of course, a magnificent specimen of a Fresnel, second order.'

That's merely an obligatory opening line. What follows makes it quickly apparent that Marsha, Nick, and I are peripheral to his remarks. We are not the ones he needs to impress.

'A radius of 700 millimetres, a height of 2,069 millimetres, and weight of 1,601 kilograms. Number built—261, number still in lighthouses at last count—125.' The stats fly deftly off his tongue. 'I myself have been to several others, as have several of you.'

'Point Bonita, San Francisco Bay,' calls out Marco. 'Wild location. The one lighthouse in the US that can only be accessed by a suspension bridge.'

'Boston Light, Little Brewster Island, outer Boston Harbour,' declares Andy, now back to himself. 'Iconic lighthouse, often called "the ideal American lighthouse," the very last one in the US to be automated.'

'*Le phare d'El Hank*, Casablanca. The tallest lighthouse in Morocco at fifty-one metres. In steps—256, if I remember correctly.'

Impressive, André, if a little boastful.

'Architecturally beautiful, but the neighbourhood was a bit sketchy. Had to watch out for pickpockets.'

Height is not everything, is it André? The only con artists around Point Amour are the seagulls. Back to the lighthouse at hand.

Calvin dives deeper. 'It was Augustin-Jean Fresnel's invention of the catadioptric lens, pulling in 87 per cent of the light generated by the circular multi-wick apparatus he designed, that allowed this beacon to project its light twenty nautical miles out to sea.'

Convex and concave lenses I know. Not too up on catadioptric.

'To quote the man himself,' adds Calvin, '"Nature has not bothered with the difficulties of analysis; it has only avoided the complication of means."'

Enough said. I let it pass me by.

'I consider the words my personal mantra.'

Really, Calvin. You meditate with that in your mind? Doesn't sound like it would do much to simplify your life.

'A very good translation,' notes André.

A mantra that works well in either language. A boost for bilingualism.

'Fresnel is one of the seventy-two French scientists whose names are inscribed in gold letters around the perimeter of the first floor of the Eiffel Tower,' adds André, unnecessarily as it turns out.

The three others nod in agreement, their smugness not totally under control. Apparently, they've all seen it.

I, too, have been to the Eiffel Tower. The Fresnel inscription was not the focus of my visit, however.

To make a long and esoteric story short, Calvin wins the undeclared competition of the lighthouse commentaries. It pays to devote an academic life to pharology.

When he has finally finished, Marsha is left somewhat at sea, so to speak. She struggles to find the right words. Anything she might possibly add suddenly seems trivial.

I'm quick to her aid. 'Thank you so very much for spending time with us. As you see, it means a great deal to actually be in the presence of such an iconic lens. Might I add, Marsha, Augustin Fresnel would be very proud to see his invention in such good hands.'

'Well said,' Calvin remarks. Try not to be patronizing, Calvin. Difficult as it is at this point.

I smile tolerantly, as tour guides find themselves doing as needed.

The pharos four want to linger of course. They photograph the Fresnel from every possible angle, whereas my attention has turned to the views out the lantern-room windows.

The shoreline in front of the lighthouse has peculiar rock formations, from this distance looking rather like cobblestones.

'Patch reefs,' Marsha informs me. 'One of the few places in the world they're found.'

This small pocket of southern Labrador continues to amaze me. Though I'm certain "patch reefs" will do nothing to lure the lads from the lantern room.

Marsha doesn't share my perspective. There is a limit on the time any one group can spend at the top of the lighthouse. Other visitors are waiting in the wings on the ground floor.

'Let's make our way back down,' she says. 'You'll no doubt want to take a look at the extraordinary 530-million-year-old geological configurations along our shoreline.'

No doubt not. But an admirable try, Marsha. She catches their lack of interest.

'There's a brew of Labrador tea waiting for everyone in the kitchen,' she says. 'Tea made from a local, wild-growing species of the rhododendron family.'

Absolutely no enticement for the pharos four.

'And juniper cookies topped with fireweed jelly,' she adds.

Andy smiles. She's got one taker.

It's the linchpin that Marsha needs. 'Off we go then,' she says. 'Follow me. Backwards down the ladder, if you please.' Nick steps nimbly to the top step, as encouragement to the others.

They have no choice. One last admiring gaze at the Fresnel, an about-face, a grip on the railing, and each begins his reluctant descent. Life is short, my friends, and there are more lighthouse destinations on your bucket lists in need of your attention.

I'm again the rear guard. Going down is less taxing for me than the climb, given I'm not about to be crushed should Andy fall. In such a scenario, it would be his pharos friends making the insurance claims.

On the landing at the bottom of the ladder, there's a significant distraction.

Marco has turned to Marsha. 'Special permission?' he mutters.

I was wrong. He hasn't given up on getting to the cat-walk. He's bent forward, peering through the now-open access. The hatch has been removed and stands to one side of the passageway.

'Yes,' answers Marsha, a slight edge of impatience in her voice.

Marco is not easily dissuaded. 'Not window cleaners, I assume?'

'Not today.' Marsha, however, is duty-bound to be amenable to lighthouse visitors. Her reticence weakens. 'We have a photographer with us, working on a special project. Shall we move on then, gentlemen? We're past our allotted time.'

'That would be Amanda Thomsen,' says André.

It surprises Marsha, of course. 'We're staying at the same B & B,' I interject.

'She must have just opened the hatch,' observes André. 'Otherwise we would have seen her from the lantern room.'

'Shall we give her a shout?' suggests Andy.

'She was expecting to see us here,' says Marco.

They're all in on the act. The next thing you know, they'll want to dodge back up the ladder and have a gawk at her taking pictures.

'We have to move on,' I tell them. 'We're far past our allotted time.' Firm and efficient. 'We're seeing her at supper, folks.'

Finally they stir, bending their heads in turn to look out the open passageway as they shuffle past it to the stairs.

Once they're in motion, it's a reasonably steady descent. Andy develops a jolting but consistent rhythm that in time gets the final two of us down the stairs and past the cluster of disgruntled visitors waiting in line.

The Labrador tea proves to be a balm for the nerves—for mine, at least. The others are significantly less keen, although the juniper cookie topped with fireweed jelly generates moderate discussion.

'This is good,' I enthuse. 'A unique topper to an extraordinary lighthouse experience.' To say nothing of sustenance for an encounter with the patch reefs.

Let's just say they find the shoreline less than overwhelming. They're more interested in looking back and up at the top of the lighthouse in hopes of catching a glimpse of Amanda somewhere along the perimeter of the catwalk.

Catwalk, rim, gallery, call it what you will, its height puts it in a class far above anything else we've seen. With its red railing matching the red of the cupola above it, the Fresnel gleaming between them, it has an undisputed presence.

'Look, there she is,' declares Marco. 'Lucky devil.'

Not from my perspective. Acrophobia? I'll admit I wouldn't be caught dead out there at that height, nothing between me and doomsday but a railing.

It would seem Amanda has no such fear. When I look up, I wonder if that's a good thing, given her odd behaviour at breakfast. To my mind she wasn't in control of herself. Her jokes sounded forced. She has some issues. A love affair gone bad? Mental issues? Possibly.

Now all the lads except Calvin are waving to the miniature figure and shouting her name. She might hear them, but of course they can't communicate. It's a pointless pursuit.

Suddenly I get it. They want to be part of her photographic record. They want her to train a telescopic lens their way and make them part of the view she is capturing from her perch. They're doing all they can to get themselves into the proposed coffee-table book.

The figure disappears shortly after their clamouring starts. It appears she's moved to the opposite side of the lighthouse. Away from the irritants.

Nick has run off to give Gaffer a break from the Durango while the rest of us linger at the shoreline. With the lighthouse looming overhead, there are final photographs to be taken, afterthoughts to be absorbed. It is, after all, the last lightship we will experience together.

It calls for a group shot—the pharos four and group leader. On his return Nick does the job with my phone, together with a selfie that adds himself and Gaffer to the mix. A select pair of photos are on their way to four inboxes within minutes, images to take with them back home. My hope is that when scrolling through their pictures at some future date, they'll each pause, and inwardly beam.

We make our way to the Durango, grab one last view of the gallant tower, and head briskly out of Point Amour.

Surprise destination: gob-smacking Red Bay, an hour up the road.

'Yet another National Historic Site. Yet another UNESCO

World Heritage Site. Often called "the first industrial complex in the New World."'

Their enthusiasm, as anticipated, is sparse. They're in withdrawal.

'Sounds commercial,' comments Marco.

'Be generous and control your indifference, my friends. We're talking sixteenth century. We're talking Basque whalers with harpoons in open bloody boats.'

My patience is not what it was. The end of the tour is within reach.

'Does the town have a good restaurant?' asks Andy. 'I'm getting hungry.'

Sweet Jesus. Must that gut of his forever take priority over astounding cultural history?

I manage to stifle it. We do need to eat. 'Yes, Andy. As a matter of fact, it does. It's called the Whalers Restaurant and it's known for its Chalupa Fish and Chips.'

'Chalupa. Never knew there was such a fish.'

Nicely done, Sebastian. Hooked him good. I smile, casually. 'The chalupa was the open boat that the Basque whalers used when harpooning right and bowhead whales.'

'I see.'

And that's not all he sees while he's munching his excellent cod and fries. The restaurant's decor is all about whaling, with whale posters, whale bones, a model of the red-tiled structure where the whale blubber was rendered into whale oil.

Yes, whale oil. I've been holding off, determined to set any connection to lighthouses aside, to make one final effort at expanding their minds beyond the single tracks into which they seem permanently embedded.

Once we're past dessert—homemade crowberry (alias blackberry) pie—and working on our coffees, I make my pitch.

'Think of it—every spring a dozen galleons with six hundred tough-as-nails men and boys would cross the Atlantic from the Basque country and show up on the southern shores of Labrador. They'd take to their chalupas, row them out from Red Bay, six men to an open boat, harpooner poised in the bow, ready to drive his lance with every last ounce of his strength into the colossal beast!'

Although I have painted a formidable picture, they continue to sip their coffees, demonstrating tepid interest. As I thought, there is only one association that will boot them out of the doldrums.

'A dead whale floats. So what do they do? They tow it ashore in Red Bay, flense the blubber, render it to oil, seal the oil in barrels. And, with the holds of the galleons chock-full, they sail madly back across the ocean, ship after ship loaded with a thousand barrels of whale oil to light the lamps of Europe!'

I pause blatantly for effect.

Mediocre response.

They've left me with no choice but to pull the ace from the deck.

'Lighthouse lamps! Including *lighthouse* lamps. Of course!'

'Very doubtful,' says Calvin. 'Not in the sixteenth century.'

The others perk. There's a collective flicker in their eyes. They like it when they think I've been caught out. Calvin, straining past the temptation to gloat, shrugs.

We move on. Out the front entrance and across the road to the site's interpretation centre.

The lads face a fresh dose of historical reality.

A preserved eight-metre-long chalupa fills much of the introductory exhibition space. A Parks Canada guide is all smiles, ignorant of the challenge she faces.

'Good day, *bonjour*. My name is Céline.'

André is super quick off the mark. '*Bonjour*.' I appreciate the new-found, albeit dubious, enthusiasm. The others, however, are in no mood to have Céline repeat her commentary in a second language. They stare at André until he reluctantly admits, 'We're all good with English, *madame.*'

And off she goes, with her well-rehearsed, animated Parks Canada account of Basques whaling in Red Bay.

The lads don't trust animated. They will draw their own conclusions about how the events that took place in Red Bay four hundred years ago fit into their personal, lighthouse-centric view of the world.

Céline senses she is not quite connecting. 'Who has questions?' she says, hoping to turn the tide.

'In your opinion, was whale oil from Red Bay ever used in lighthouses?' asks Calvin, glancing at me.

She looks at André. 'You no doubt know *le roi des phares, le phare des rois.*'

André struggles to look as if he hasn't been caught by surprise. He stutters the translation—'the king of lighthouses, the lighthouse of kings'—and scans his comrades in an effort to draw attention away from himself.

'*Le phare de Cordouan,*' injects Calvin, his pronunciation a blur. 'I know it. The oldest active lighthouse in France by far.'

France, really? And André was in the dark on that one. Not quite so in the know on *les phares* as he's led us to believe.

'And,' says Céline, 'a UNESCO World Heritage Site, *comme nous.*' She glances at André. 'One of only two lighthouses in the world to have that designation.'

'And the only lighthouse in all of France that's still manned year-round,' adds know-it-all Calvin.

'Exactly,' says Céline. She figures she's on to something. 'We know construction of the lighthouse began in 1584. We know production of whale oil didn't end in Red Bay until the early 1600s. Therefore, yes, it is possible that whale oil from Red Bay lit the oldest lighthouse in France.'

I love it. Vindication is sweet. All eyes are on Calvin. Mine are accompanied by a slight smile.

Calvin is saying nothing. He's not looking at us. He's on his phone. 'Ha,' he finally retorts. 'The original light came from, and I quote, "burning oak chips in a metal container." Ha!'

Killjoy. Pure and simple.

'And get this.' He's practically wetting his pants. '"In 1645, the wood-fired lantern was blown off by a storm and replaced by a new lantern designed to burn whale oil." 1645!'

There's no need, Calvin. You made your point. Gloating, no matter how late in the game, is still nasty.

'Nevertheless,' says Andy, 'it's conceivable. It could be left-over whale oil. In storage since the barrels arrived from Red Bay.'

Andy, my man, forget any disparaging thoughts I ever had about you.

Of course, Calvin is far from convinced. The others, however, are willing to entertain the possibility.

A stalemate. So be it. Three out of four ain't bad.

Plus it has aroused enough interest that the pharos four spend a solid thirty minutes venturing through the displays. I call that progress, a definite expansion of brain capacity beyond the beacon towers.

All good things, however, must come to an end. It's soon time to hit the road back to our B & B in Forteau, take a couple of hours of downtime to reflect and refuel before we head off to the Florian.

I'm smiling behind the steering wheel. I do not recall ever anticipating the final, tour-ending meal with quite the same enthusiasm.

I pump up the music, head bopping to the lighthouse beat.

IN THE LIGHT

THE MUSIC HAS come to an end. All is surprisingly quiet. I suspect they are ruminating on what the last ten days have brought. I'm betting that in at least one of the pharos four there's sprung the urge to take to Tripadvisor and spew a few complimentary phrases. While, at the same time, momentum is building for the four of them to chip in and purchase a bottle of champagne and, around the fire tonight with glasses in hand, offer a robust toast in celebration of "an extraordinary tour and its spirited leader." (To quote a participant from a previous expedition.)

I have known a concluding night to turn embarrassingly sappy and sentimental. To be honest, I can't see it happening in this case. Nonetheless, a bottle of champagne would not go astray.

We are nearing the access road that earlier in the day took us to Point Amour. The lighthouse is not visible from this distance, but that doesn't stop a collective turn of the heads in its direction, followed not long after by faint humming rising in the air behind me, growing gradually louder and louder.

Their inhibitions have totally fallen away. The three

pharologists and one *pharologue* have joined forces and are now loudly humming one of the playlist favourites, "You Light Up My Life."

My ears don't lie. They have taken their obsession to a new and extraordinarily cheesy level.

Pharos four—you light up my life in ways you didn't anticipate. You've set the bar of eccentric clientele very high. The stories will be told long after you've gone.

By the time we arrive at the Grenfell B & B, their spirits have eased back to near normal. Who knows what's ahead once their batteries have been recharged?

Andy's cell rings as soon as we go inside. He heads to his room. 'Yes, Maude, I'm remembering to take the medication,' he says into the phone. Then, just before opening his door, 'Yes. It's under control.' He shuts the door behind him.

It's clearly not an appetite suppressant he's talking about.

The others retire to their rooms, except Marco, who comes looking for me in the sitting room as I'm easing into a dram and making notes in my tour folder.

He has a question. 'Do you mind if I borrow the vehicle? I'd like to take a run into Blanc Sablon to the liquor outlet.'

'No problem.'

I smell something *extraordinaire* from the vineyards of Champagne. Maybe he'll even pick up a wedge or two of exceptional cheese. Olives stuffed with anchovies? Oysters? A couple of baguettes to toast around the fire and top with foie gras?

I check the time. It's almost 5:45. 'Just remember our dinner reservation is at seven.' I hand him the keys. And off he goes with my unreserved blessing.

In such close proximity to the Quebec border, the food and drink cravings are intense. I say we'll be singing in French before the night is out. Ha! How about *Au clair de la lune*? From Nick's French kindergarten.

The joie de vivre dissipates. All's quiet. Nick is off walking Gaffer. I'm thinking I might just fit in a short nap myself. Before stretching out on the sofa, I drop a chummy text to Mae. And one to Amanda, to make sure she's still on for this evening. I thought maybe she'd be back at the B & B by now. There's a quick reply: she's still at the lighthouse. She'll come to the restaurant straight from there.

Waiting on the perfect light conditions, I'm thinking. I doze off.

After I've lain comatose for an unspecified period, a dog leaping onto my chest jerks me back to life. 'Gaffer!' The mutt has no tact.

'Sorry about that,' says Nick.

The laughter says otherwise. I upright myself and check my phone.

'You were gone a long time.'

'Went past the Florian, as far as Buckle's Point.'

'Good walk?'

'You know Gaffer. He gets off on rocks and water. I think I saw André, in the parking lot of the Florian. I couldn't be sure. The guy was leaning over, talking to someone in a car.'

'Really? He must have gone for a walk, if it was him.'

'That guy loves to talk. Especially if he happens to run into someone from Quebec.'

Which reminds me. 'Nick, I have a question. Do you know any French campfire songs?'

Upping the chance of a Tripadvisor review in French. My first. Could prove useful.

It takes the lad a few seconds, but he finally catches up to his father's train of thought. 'You mean like sitting around the fire after we get back from supper?'

'Right.'

'Like summer camp, only we're all chuggin' a few beer?'

A year and a bit from the legal drinking age. The young fellow gets a charge out of testing the waters.

'Not *all* of us.'

'I know, I know. Some of us prefer Scotch.'

Not only is he now taller than I am, he thinks he's quicker on the uptake.

'You like to try some?'

That stops him in his tracks.

'Really?'

'We're practically in Quebec. Where the drinking age is eighteen. You're close enough.'

'You serious?'

'I could be. Parental decision. Controlled circumstance. A small dram. What do you think?'

His reaction is curious. I expected him to be all over it. He's hinted at this moment for years. A game, of course, never expecting me to give in. Suddenly his old man has called his bluff. He fights to keep his cool.

'Why not?'

It's Laphroaig. Brine, peat, iodine and seaweed. Someone once described Laphroaig as licking smoke-tanned leather while running naked through a field of barley. The kid doesn't know what he's in for. I'm fully awake and about to savour a very interesting moment.

I return from the kitchen, small glass in hand. I pour just enough for him to taste, on the assumption he'll likely upchuck it into the glass.

'Here you go. This'll put hairs on your chest.' I'm smiling as I hand it to him. I raise my own glass in a toast. 'Cheers!'

'Slàinte Mhath!'

I'd forgotten I'd once told him the Gaelic equivalent. He lifts the glass to the light and gently swirls it around. 'Nice colour. Good legs.'

Where did he pick that up? From me? Not something I usually do.

He sinks his nose into the glass. Takes a lungful before emerging. 'Gotta love that peat. And medicinal, absolutely.' He pauses. 'A hospital gone up in smoke.'

Clever, very clever. He's been rehearsing this for years. Let's see what happens when he actually tastes it.

A small, calculated sip. He swirls it around in his mouth. No intake of air, which means he's not tasting anything. But he has to swallow sooner or later. Here it comes.

Discreet gulp. The wait. The anticipation.

The bugger licks his lips. 'Not quite so strong as I expected, and not very subtle. I'd give it a 7.5 out of 10.' He's the one smiling.

Okay. I hand it to him. He pulled that off. Or thinks he did. Smoke and mirrors, if you ask me. Which makes me think he's probably been into a bottle at my place when I haven't been around.

'Not your first time, by the look of it.'

'A few months ago. Off and on. Curious, that's all.'

I don't say anything. Which is as good as saying I'm not impressed.

'You're surprised?'

'Maybe not. Should I be?'

'Dad, man, I'd have told you if you'd asked. I wasn't about to get drunk. Just wanted to see why you get so pumped about the stuff. Actually, I didn't like much of it.'

A brain that's not only sharp, but damn practical. I'm left struggling.

'The Glenmorangie was not bad. But I'll hold off on the rest.'

He even pronounced it correctly. What's there to say? 'Scotch is an acquired taste.' It's the best I can do.

Fortunately, Andy shows up.

It's six-thirty. He's wearing a diamond-patterned sweater vest over a white shirt, dress pants, leather shoes. His grey hair has not a single strand out of place. He's prepared to eat a horse but groomed to do it with class.

'Have a seat, Andy. Just waiting on the others.'

Which prompts me to head to my room and get my own self in shape for the restaurant. On my way back I check the parking lot. Vacant. No sign of Marco.

Calvin and André, energized but lacking Andy's spark, have also shown up in the sitting room.

'Out for a walk, André?'

He's surprised by the question. 'Not me.'

Nick says nothing. I leave it at that.

We're all waiting on Marco. The Florian Restaurant is only a few minutes away, but it's already 6:50. Either he had difficulty deciding on the champagne or he lost track of time.

Or he's had an accident. It suddenly hits me that he's not covered by the rental agreement. I didn't add any secondary drivers to the insurance.

I'm just about to fire off a text when I hear the spit of gravel. And, sure enough, there he is, in under the wire.

'Sorry about that,' he says, heading for the kitchen. He stuffs the carry bag in the fridge without unpacking it.

He dashes off to his room but doesn't stay there any longer than it would take to brush and gargle. He joins us at the front entrance, looking no different than he did when he arrived. Definitely the least shipshape of us all.

The five minutes inside the Durango is hardly time enough to confirm that something is up with Marco, but his continued reticence once inside the restaurant leaves no question in my mind. He says nothing, even as he pockets two twenty-dollar bills that Calvin slips to him, money I assume Calvin had borrowed at some point in the tour.

I purposely sit next to Marco. The chair on his other side is vacant. We're waiting on Amanda.

He pretends to be studying the menu. Whenever we've sat down to a meal before, he's never taken this long without joining in the banter about the food choices.

He finally looks up. 'I'll go with the cod.'

'You mean the sautéed fillet topped with Basque *piperade* sauce on basmati rice with pea puree.' Just to make a point.

He's not amused. It escapes the others, who are still bantering. Their eventual choices make it an all-seafood fest—crab, scallops, smoked char, shrimp, blackened halibut, and, of course, the Basque cod. We wait to order. All the while indulging in the pinot grigio just delivered to the table, looking through a bank of tall windows over open fields edged by trees and leading to a rugged coastline. There is only one thing missing.

Amanda.

A half-hour has passed since we arrived at the restaurant. We've held off ordering our meals, thinking she would arrive at any minute. She doesn't. I drop her a text. There's no response.

'She's driving,' Calvin suggests. 'She doesn't want to take time to pull over to the side of the road.'

'It doesn't explain why she wouldn't have let us know she was going to be late.'

'Her phone could have died.'

'Or her car broke down.'

'Or she just lost track of time.'

None of which comes from Marco. He notices I notice.

'I think we should go ahead and eat,' he says.

I don't disagree. They should go ahead at least. 'You guys order, while I take a quick jaunt to the lighthouse. Just to check. Who knows, maybe she had an accident. Won't take me long, a half-hour max. Chances are I'll meet her on the way, in which case we'll be back sooner.'

Not quite how we had planned to start off the evening, but there it is. No arguments. I take a sip of white wine and push back from the table.

'Want me to come with you, Dad?'

'I'm good. Tell the waiter I'll have the smoked char. I'll text you when I leave to come back, so it'll be ready when I get here. I'll text Amanda's order while I'm at it.'

I cut out and make for the Durango. I'm met with a bark.

Gaffer's been aroused from his sleep, having made quick work of his confinement treats. I move him and his safety restraint to the front passenger seat and we're off.

The highway's quiet, meaning her green Mini Cooper is not going to escape me, should it show up from the opposite direction. I reach the access road in short order. Despite the gravel road, it's not long to L'Anse Amour.

I love this time of the year, with its long evenings. The light catches the shoreline—not spectacular, certainly striking. As I drive on, what's spectacular is the bank of billowy cumulus clouds set against the blue sky beyond the lighthouse. An outstanding backdrop for a photographer. Perhaps that explains Amanda's delay.

Her car is in the parking lot—a big relief. I had thoughts of her rushing back late, careening off the highway and over an embankment.

Hers is the sole vehicle in the lot. She was given permission to remain in the lighthouse after closing, I assume, considering her project is backed by the same association that operates the lighthouse.

I exit the Durango with an excited Gaffer on a tight leash, stopping soon after as my eyes scale the tower to the catwalk. I half expect Amanda to be there, taking pictures, somehow capturing a reflection of the sky in the lantern-room windows.

Not so. At least not on this side of the tower. I walk on to the door of the main entrance of the lighthouse, wondering if it might have been left open. No such luck. Amanda must have locked it from the inside.

How to go about getting her attention? I pound on the door with my fist a few times, before concluding it's a useless exercise. Undoubtedly she's so far up the tower that any such noise is out of hearing range.

I need to get myself in her sightline. Which means heading to the opposite side of the tower, pulling back from its base and the gravel path that circles the lighthouse, all the while yelling skyward, in the hope that she is indeed on the catwalk and will hear me. Gaffer, faithful assistant, joins in with a succession of sharp yelps.

'Amanda!' Several times. No response.

I move along a bit further, to where the lighthouse faces the open ocean, all the time giving my lungs a full-strength work-out. 'Amanda!' I'm starting to feel like an idiot. Gaffer, on the other hand, is energized by the sudden freedom of unrestricted barking.

We've not gone far when we're face to face with the fence that encloses the back of the lighthouse property. Beyond it, the land drops away to the shoreline. Unless I jump the fence, I can't move far enough away from the lighthouse to get a good view of the catwalk. In which case Amanda won't see me unless she looks over its railing and straight down. I mutter in frustration.

Gaffer is not so easily put off. His barking intensifies. He tugs wildly on his leash, jerking me away from the fence and further along the path. Abruptly, he digs in all four paws.

'What the—?'

I recoil. Sweet Jesus.

Shattered face-first on the path, feet touching the base of the lighthouse. Shattered and sunk into coarse gravel. Arms splayed as if to lessen the impact. Hopeless, twisted limbs, extending from what can only be a mass of broken bones. And a mass of vital organs crushed against the body wall. Blood-soaked gravel, the clearest, most unremarkable evidence of death.

No need to step closer. She is a stark, barbaric corpse.

Her battered camera lies nearby.

I shrink from the scene, reeling, heart-stricken, back to the vehicle. I set Gaffer inside. I lean my back against the closed door and breathe deeply several times. I call 911.

There will be a wait. But not a long one. The nearest RCMP detachment is in Forteau.

I walk to the rear of the Durango and open the liftgate. I dig about to locate the first-aid kit and from it remove a package of latex gloves.

The return to the corpse is fraught with indecision. There has been an inner emotional change. From tour guide to investigator. And with it the urge to seek any piece of evidence whatsoever that might help me understand why the young woman came to her death in this way.

As gruelling as it is to stand and take pictures with my phone, it might, in some yet unknown way, prove useful. Even if the cause of death is suicide.

I have a gut feeling it is. Yet the possibility exists that it is not.

Which is why I encase my hands in the latex gloves. Why I step toward her camera and bend over it.

The hesitation takes a few moments to overcome. I lift the camera from its depression in the gravel.

The camera declares itself to be a Nikon, a D850. The lens is cracked. The monitor, which seemingly could be tilted, has broken away from the camera body. The battery cover has popped open, and the battery pack lies on the ground not far away.

What tempts me is the memory card. What holds me back from sliding open the slot cover and retrieving it is the fact that I have no way to read the card and return it to its slot before the cops arrive.

I'm thinking my methodology is off. There must be another way.

If one cover has popped, why not another. Why not popped when the camera hit the ground and the memory card went flying. Or better yet—the camera struck the railing of the catwalk, the cover burst open, and who knows where the hell the memory card ended up.

All possibilities. All possibilities that could lead me to tampering with evidence. Evidence that, if the memory card yielded significant images, I would have to somehow make sure it got into the hands of the RCMP. At which point I could end up in deeper shit than I could ever work myself out of.

As tempting as it is, I can only conclude it's not worth the risk. I set the camera back on the gravel.

RCMP crime scene investigators have eyes like hawks. If the camera has been disturbed, they'll know it. Unless someone was smart enough to take a picture with his iPhone of the evidence lying on the gravel, then use it to set the evidence back into the depression. In the exact same spot, with its strap curling in the exact same way.

Where, less than two metres away, is lying a horrifying corpse.

Most private investigators will sometimes lose themselves in the moment, unintentionally allowing the desperation to get to the cause of death to override the horror at the inhumanity of the scene. Unfortunately, the more cases PIs deal with, the more prone they are to such a lapse. Some would call it stone-heartedness and rationalize that it comes with the territory. That it's a necessity, even, if you want to survive in the business.

I, on the other hand, now find myself retreating to the fence, leaning over it, and throwing up my guts. Or attempting to. Precisely expressed as the dry heaves.

Which reminds me to text Nick at the restaurant. Once I get a partial grip on myself.

Longer than expected. Not to worry. Back in touch soon. No details to cause alarm.

Order your meal?

Hold off.

Another dry heave. The final one before the sound of tires spitting gravel.

The RCMP have arrived. The car halts at the main entrance just as I get there. Quick exit. Quick exchange of names. Corporal Larsen. Corporal Beauchamp. More dirt flying as we launch ourselves in the direction of the body.

They charge past me, responding to their urgent expectation that something can be done to save a life. I'm afraid not.

By the time I catch up and stand between them, they have come to terms with what has happened. Unnerved. Close to shell-shocked. No indication of ever having encountered such a scene before.

'From the very top of the lighthouse—thirty-three metres. From the catwalk—close to thirty.'

They're not ready for cold statistics. They look straight up and conclude for themselves that the plunge down gave the person zero chance of survival.

'You know the woman, Mr. Synard?' asks Corporal Larsen.

'Amanda Thomsen.'

Given the full name, divulged so swiftly, he expects more. The corporal has turned bluntly professional.

The man is in his early thirties at the most, at least twenty years younger than I am. His years as an officer I could likely count on two hands. As for Corporal Beauchamp, likely one. Nevertheless, they stare at me until I fall in line.

Out comes all there is to tell. How I came to know her. Why I showed up at the lighthouse when I did. Precious little to recount, really. I've known Amanda Thomsen for barely twenty-four hours.

'Quite likely suicide,' I suggest to Corporal Larsen, who appears to wield more authority than his teammate. 'The light-house narrows considerably from the base to the catwalk. Looks to me like she leapt to avoid hitting the wall on the way down.'

He doesn't respond. To speculate with a civilian is firmly outside his professional boundaries.

It's obvious there are only two possibilities. Suicide or foul play. Either she jumped or she was pushed. Despite what I just said, I will remain open to pushed. But I know that's definitely not the place to start with the RCMP.

'She could have been leaning over to get a good shot and fell.' That too. But to my mind that doesn't jibe with the way the body hit the ground.

Corporal Larsen takes out his phone and steps away. I continue to speculate. He's likely attempting to get through to Marsha, head of the lighthouse staff, there when the lighthouse closed to the public this afternoon and Amanda was allowed to stay inside alone. Indeed, Marsha could very likely be the last person to see Amanda Thomsen alive.

Or she could just as likely not be. From what I saw of Amanda, she didn't necessarily play by the rules.

I suspect the corporal is also on his phone to call in a forensic team to pore over the scene. The area surrounding the lighthouse will have to be cordoned off, and a perimeter established around the corpse. Something brought in to cover it, waterproof sheeting at least. A tent covering the perimeter will likely have to wait until forensics show up.

In the meantime, Corporal Beauchamp is looking increasing lacklustre. I'd suggest a trip to the fence but that could be seen as insinuating he's not up to the task at hand.

Being left to ruminate on what that task might be is exacerbating his condition. He's made a brief entry in his notebook (time of day and location, presumably) and is now in standby mode. He avoids direct focus on the maimed and disfigured for fear of throwing up his guts.

Yet he appears unsure whether he should be engaging with me in conversation, even though it might prove a distraction and an antidote to his nausea.

I will at least try. 'Where's home for you, Corporal?'

The young man is still unsure, as trivial as the question is. In the end his gut lurches, he gags, and he gives in. 'Flin Flon.'

Very good. 'And people tell us we have strange placenames. To me Flin Flon, Manitoba, is right up there with Dildo, Newfoundland. I mean, set aside the sexual connotation (hard to do, I know) and you'd find that Dildo is from an Englishman trying to get his tongue around *île d'eau*.'

It's turned the corporal's mind away from his stomach.

'I've always wondered how Flin Flon got its name.' I haven't really, but the corporal has brightened considerably.

'Named after a character in a science fiction novel—Josiah Flintabbatey Flonatin.'

Now then. That eased out of him quite comfortably. I push on. 'There's a story, no doubt.'

'A prospector was reading the book when he discovered a copper deposit. Named the mine after the character. He shortened it, of course.'

'As you would.' I'm pleased to see a promising spark of enthusiasm. 'To live in a place called Forteau must seem rather mundane to you. By comparison.'

He doesn't quite get the humour. No matter, his mind is off the corpse.

Unfortunately, the officer's superior returns and sets his mind right back on it again. 'Forensics will be arriving from Corner Brook tomorrow. They should make the ten-thirty ferry. In the meantime, Corporal Beauchamp, we'll need stakes and barrier tape. And plastic sheeting to cover the body.'

Corporal Beauchamp is happy enough to be heading back to the police vehicle to retrieve them. I might not, however, be around to witness him putting them to use.

Corporal Larsen hands me a card with the contact info for the Forteau detachment. He records my cell number. When it comes to my place of residence, a complication arises.

'You're due to check out from the B & B at what time?'

'We're booked on the one o'clock ferry.'

'That may not be possible. We need a detailed statement. It may have consequences. I'm expecting you to be at the detachment first thing in the morning.'

By which he means that at this point, I'm central to the investigation. But also means he doesn't understand that I have a schedule to follow to get the tour group to Deer Lake to catch their flights.

There is no point in arguing with the RCMP, especially at this stage of the game. My statement will make very clear the full extent of my contact with the deceased. It will detail every last scrap of information I have about Amanda Thomsen, as sparse as it is.

'The detachment opens at eight-thirty.'

'I'll be knocking at your door.' With prepared statement in hand that will clear the way for me to get the tour back up and running, on time.

I board the Durango. 'Sorry about that, pal.' Gaffer is not particularly impressed at having to wait so long, but a few treats and all is forgiven. I text Nick.

Hey pal. Sorry about the wait. OMW.

He's not so easily mollified. *We finished dessert! What's going on?*

Change my meal to takeout. Picking up everyone asap. Will explain.

They meet me at the front entrance to the restaurant. I edge past them to collect the takeout and pay the bill.

The evening is askew. They're burning for an explanation. It will have to wait until we're back at the B & B. Until I have their focused, collective attention. I turn in the driver's seat, setting forth a positive vibe. 'Everyone enjoy their meal?'

Brooding enthusiasm. Only then do I notice an empty seat. 'What's with Marco?'

'He decided to walk back. He skipped dessert.'

When we arrive at the B & B there's Marco, sitting by the firepit, well-fed flames lighting the Adirondack chairs circling it. On an arm of each of them is a wine glass and in Marco's hands is a bottle.

'Have a seat.' He cuts away the foil that caps the bottle, then releases its wire cage. He uses both thumbs to pressure the naked cork . . . and up it flies, arcing into the fire.

Champagne. As predicted.

Marco walks from chair to chair, pouring as he goes. When he's finished, he raises his own glass. 'Here's to us. Lucky buggers. Excellent tour.'

I stand up and position myself behind the chair so everyone has a clear view of their tour guide.

'Way to go, Sebastian,' Marco adds.

I raise my left hand to quell any more accolades that might be coming my way. 'Tonight . . . I want us all to raise our glasses in tribute to one unforgettable individual.' It's a daunting task but I take a deep breath and press ahead. 'A person we knew only briefly, and who, to my mind, was a troubled soul. To Amanda Thomsen. May she rest in peace.'

It is not the most conventional of ways to inform them of her death, but perhaps fitting. Unconventional herself, Amanda would have approved, I think.

To a person they're absolutely stunned. Plainly, quietly, I inform them of what has taken place.

'There was something odd about her,' Calvin says after it sinks in. 'We can only assume she was struggling with her demons.'

'I found her refreshing, to be honest,' says André. '*Exceptionnelle*. Her mind was her own.'

I don't quite know where that's coming from, given his brief contact with her.

'I noticed she always had something on her mind, even when she was eating.' That would be Andy.

I look at Nick. He has nothing to add, which leads me to think he's struggling to figure out what he thought of her.

Which leaves Marco. He's stiff, seemingly disoriented. His relationship with Amanda must have been stronger than I had realized. Which now makes me think he probably did spend last night with her.

Marco rises from his chair, turns, and leaves. Not a word, no eye contact with any of us.

What do we say to that? Blank faces, collective perplexity.

And a long silence. Each of us attempting to come to terms with what has happened.

In the end, Andy is the one to break the silence. 'Any champagne left in the bottle?'

As good a next move as any, I suppose. I retrieve the bottle from the arm of Marco's chair and hold it up to the firelight.

Not much, but a little for each of us.

'It was very good of Marco,' says André. 'A good sparkling wine.'

I check the label, angling it toward the fire to read. 'Cuvée Catharine Brut. Sounds like champagne.'

André smiles indulgently.

My phone's light sweeps the label. He's right. '*Vin mousseux.*'

Nick corrects my pronunciation and translates. Unnecessarily.

André wouldn't outdo me on Scotch, but the fellow knows his wine.

'I'm surprised he didn't buy a good *blanc de blancs* in Blanc Sablon,' he says.

Not exactly sure what you're talking about, André, but sounding clever nonetheless.

'I would think the SAQ carries a decent bottle at a good price,' he adds. 'Of course, it can't be called Champagne if it doesn't come from the Champagne *appellation* of France.'

I expect I knew that. In any case, put it behind us. There's more than wine on our minds.

'How awful was it, really,' asks Calvin, 'to discover the body? The impact had to be horrific.'

'You must have been nauseated,' says Andy.

'I dealt with it.'

'I would have barfed big time,' he says, both brutally and boorishly honest.

No comment. I suggest we call it a day and, as hard as it might be, try to get a decent night's sleep.

But not before the owner of the B & B shows up, frantic after hearing from the RCMP.

'Dear Lord, you've heard then. How awful.' Peggy's in tears. Nothing this dreadful has happened in the area in years, let alone to anyone in any way associated with her B & B.

I try to put it in perspective. 'There's nothing you could have done. The young woman was very upset with her life, for whatever reason.'

'But she seemed perfectly fine. Didn't you think so?'

'One never knows what is going on beneath the surface. Some people can put on a very brave face.'

It does little to calm her. She's looking for answers. At this point there are none.

This is where Mae would have been a great help. The women would have been hugging each other the moment Peggy arrived. What I have to offer is a genuine, if somewhat stiff, embrace. It's not quite spontaneous.

Peggy turns to go in the house, hardly calmer than when she arrived, but changes her mind and returns to her vehicle. 'I'll see you at breakfast,' I call to her.

This is the dilemma. Had Amanda been a close friend, a broader range of emotion would come into play. Each of our relationships amounted to a brief acquaintance with the young woman. Her death was no less tragic, but I anticipate that, within a few days, it will be set aside and we will move on.

I come to this conclusion alone in the sitting room over reheated smoked char. And when that settles, a modest dram. Computer on my lap, I begin drafting the statement that will accompany me to the RCMP detachment in the morning.

Precise and clear, without missing a detail. Given that there are very few, it doesn't take long to complete. Tomorrow, when I get it printed at the RCMP detachment, it will fill less than a single page.

Nick wanders in just as I close the computer and set it aside. I had hoped he'd manage to doze off.

'Sad. Very sad,' he says, adding quickly, 'Are you all right?'

'I'm fine.'

He sits next to me on the sofa. 'You want to talk about it?'

Reversing roles, it sounds like to me. I'm touched by the thoughtfulness. I lean over and give him a hug.

'Not really.'

'I can understand.'

There's silence. For a while an agreed-to, practical silence.

Now I'm not so sure it's the right choice. 'You have something you want to say?'

'Maybe. I don't have to.' He waits only a moment. 'I don't think it was suicide. I think she was more confident in herself than you give her credit for.'

At his age, he hasn't had enough life experience to be so definite in his conclusion. I'm thinking it's best, though, if I just go along with him.

'You could be right. The RCMP will have talked to her family by now. They likely know a lot we don't.'

'Say it wasn't suicide. Wouldn't you be fired up to find out who did it?'

Fired up? He's used to seeing me jump into investigative mode. When the situation warrants it. In this instance, I'm more than happy to let the RCMP do their job and, as I see it, work their way to the conclusion that Amanda Thomsen was troubled enough that she took her own life.

'Possibly. Let's just say I have to focus on getting the four guys to Deer Lake in time to catch their flights. And meeting up with Mae for our holiday. Which reminds me, I need to make arrangements to get you and Gaffer back to St. John's. Make sure I call your mother tomorrow. I'm thinking the DRL bus from Deer Lake. I wonder if they take dogs.'

It succeeds in getting past his single focus. 'I doubt it. I could fly.'

'Big bucks.'

'Can't be that much. One way ticket. No more than an hour.'

You would think. But air travel within Newfoundland? Like I said, big bucks. On short notice—bigger bucks.

He retrieves his phone. 'Hey Siri, what is the cheapest flight tomorrow, one way, Deer Lake, Newfoundland, to St. John's, Newfoundland?'

It doesn't take Siri long. 'I found this on the web.'

A link shows up on his screen. He punches in the details. 'Tomorrow would cost . . .' Hesitating, no doubt, because he can't believe his eyes. 'Five hundred and four dollars and ninety-nine cents.'

'Plus the cost of sending Gaffer, who is too big to go as carry-on and would be traumatized in the baggage compartment. Out of the question.'

'I'm good with the bus.'

Back to his phone. 'As I suspected: "Absolutely no animals or other pets of any kind are allowed on the bus." That leaves Gaffer to find his own way home.'

'That we'll deal with later.' Meaning it looks like Mae and I are stuck with the mutt. 'Right now, you need a good night's sleep.'

He's about to wander off, back to the room, another life lesson learned. Not before he gives me another hug. 'You too, Dad. Don't be staying up too late. The Scotch is not worth it.'

Love that kid. What did I do to deserve him in my life? Despite all that's happened in the last few hours, there's a lot right with the world. I'll just ease my way through what's left in the glass, turn out the lights in the sitting room, and make my own way to bed.

Not before catching a glimpse of a still fully dressed Marco, on his way to the kitchen. He's obviously not yet in sleep mode. I retreat into the darkened room. Do I really want to get into a conversation with him? Squelch what peace of mind I've managed to gain? I'd rather just wait until he finishes his foray to the kitchen and ambles back to his room. I'll deal with him in the morning.

The refrigerator door is opened and closed. Followed by the hiss of a can's tab. Hardly a surprise. I'm hoping he doesn't decide to head to the sitting room to drink it.

He has another location in mind. He exits through the front door. I venture to a window and draw back its curtain, just enough to steal a look outside. The light over the front steps reveals him seated in one of chairs around the cold firepit. Beer in one hand, his illuminated cellphone in the other.

I leave him to it. He has the ride to Deer Lake to catch up on his sleep.

I, on the other hand, have a long and wakeful day ahead, starting with what I'm counting on to be a quick, perfunctory face-to-face with Corporal Larsen. Time to get the pharos four back on home territory, deliver Nick back to the welcoming hands of his mother, and break the news to Gaffer that his days of Durango confinement are not yet over.

And time to welcome Mae back into my life, to slip into a much-needed relaxing vacation that will clear the mind of the tour guide's preoccupations and reposition it toward something both uplifting and sublime. Just the thought of it brightens me.

Let's not go there. I need my sleep.

BLINDED BY THE LIGHT

THE TOUR-ENDING DAY dawns and I'm up, showered, shaved, and seated alone at the breakfast table.)

Peggy has only just arrived. 'You're up early,' she says, her words lacking their usual spark.

'I'm meeting with Corporal Larsen.'

'He asked me to keep her room locked. Officers will be coming around to search it sometime today. I find it all so upsetting to have Mounties on the premises, doing whatever it is they do.'

'Peggy, do you mind if I offer a few words, as someone who's worked as a private investigator, who's observed police procedures for years?'

It takes some time for her to get her mind around the fact I could be anything but a tour guide.

'Only in the off-season.' That might put it in a perspective she can handle.

I'm not sure it does. She's already burnt the toast. When she delivers her second attempt, replenishing my coffee at the same time, she decides to join me, pouring a cup for herself.

'What's your advice?'

'It'll take time, but let it play out,' I tell her. 'The police need to be thorough or they're not doing their job.'

'But what could they possibly be looking for?'

'Anything that would help them confirm it was suicide. Books she might have been reading. Medications she might have been taking. A suicide note, of course, although most people don't leave them.'

'It all sounds so cut and dried,' Peggy says, shaking her head. 'The Amanda I knew seemed unusually eager to experience life, not deny it.'

I don't say it, but no one can make a sound judgment about a person based on a couple of hours of contact.

'She stayed here twice before. She was always so positive.'

Even so, a total of three short stays. Nowhere near enough time to grasp the depth of someone's innermost emotions.

'When she was here last week, she was in a serious relationship that seemed to be going well.'

Peggy is trying hard to put a positive spin on Amanda. She's being kind.

Hard to be both kind and objective. Let's be realistic—a twenty-something in a relationship doesn't say much. Serious or otherwise, it's par for the course.

Peggy has her opinion. I try not to discredit it. 'Could be the relationship soured,' I suggest.

'I didn't sense it had.'

Nor did she sense it hadn't.

It's best to stop at that.

'She already booked her next stay, for herself and her mom. Her mom was going to fly in from St. John's for a few days. A mother-daughter time-out, she called it.'

'When is the booking?'

Peggy checks her computer. 'July 12 to 14, Amanda and Astrid Thomsen.'

Okay. So Amanda Thomsen was planning ahead. Or

pretending to be planning ahead. Making her life seem as normal as possible. Questions: what's actually been going on with this so-called boyfriend? A hiatus in a "serious relationship" to fit in a costly "time-out" with the mother? Doesn't sound entirely well-adjusted to me.

I need to conclude the breakfast chat. No way am I about to change the woman's mind. It will take the police investigation to do that.

I check the time. I'll be a bit early at the police station, but Larsen was undoubtedly up at the crack of dawn, eyes and ears into the investigation. Besides the fact that the quicker I get this over with, the less stress I'll have in making it to the ferry on time.

By 8:15 I'm up the front steps of the detachment and trying the door. It's firmly locked. My choice is to kill fifteen minutes, knock loudly, or turn aside and phone the number on the card I've just retrieved from my wallet.

No one answers. It goes to three options. No, it's not an emergency. And no, I do not want to report an incident requiring a police response that is not an emergency. I frustratingly fall under "general enquiries." Five rings and no answer. I disconnect and call again. I aim to sound persistent.

On the third try the door opens behind me. 'Good morning,' announces an intent Corporal Larsen. 'We picked you up on the monitor. You're persistent.' He checks his watch. 'And twelve minutes early.'

That said, he stands aside to let me in. With preliminaries out of the way, it's down to business. I barely have time to acknowledge Corporal Beauchamp and to note that his colour is much improved. I'm soon seated inside Corporal Larsen's office and looking across his desk as he opens a file.

'There's the matter of your statement of course, but before we get to that, I need your take on an image.'

Image? Need my take? I like the sense of camaraderie, but I'm lacking context here.

'It's from the memory card of her camera. It would be the last picture she took before the fall.'

The temptation that I allowed to pass me by. Now I'm certain I made the right decision.

'You being a PI and all.'

I stiffen, slightly. Surprised. But I shouldn't be.

'I just got off the phone with the detachment on Fogo Island. They filled me in.'

A murder case from last year. I should have learned by now not to underestimate the databases of the RCMP.

He does a few quick procedures on his laptop, then rotates it so I'm face to face with the screen.

I work at making sense of what I see. There are two red bars, angled vertically. It must be the red railing of the catwalk, shot with the camera in an unnatural position. Beyond that there's what I take (when I twist my head) to be ocean and cloud-filled sky, divided by a faint horizon line.

And at the bottom of the picture there's something blocking what would have been more red railing. I'm having trouble figuring out exactly what it is.

Larsen turns the laptop back to himself, performs one function and turns it my way again. He's rotated the image. Close to what it would have been had the camera been level with the railing.

The aberrant object, now shifted to the right side, is out of focus and fills roughly a quarter of the screen. I still can't make sense of it.

'Do you see hair on skin?' says the corporal. 'Possibly a fore-arm?'

I lean forward, closer to the screen. 'Yes, I suppose it could be.' Could be, but far from the only choice.

'And what's that?' He points. "On the wrist?'

If it is a wrist. A band of some kind? 'Mind if I play around with the image.'

'What do you mean?'

Maybe not the best choice of words. 'Edit. Make a few adjustments to the lighting.'

'Go ahead. Just be sure you can bring it back to normal.'

He knows less about digital photography than I do. These days there's no such thing as normal. It's all about manipulating the image to whatever works best for the photographer. A personal beef of mine. Making the landscape look better than it does with the naked eye. I digress.

I enlarge the "wrist," then take the image into edit mode. I work with the exposure and contrast, then heighten the colour.

I stare at the results. Unexpectedly my fingers stiffen and pull back from the keyboard. Is that what I think it might be?

I look up at Larsen. 'Shit.' Terse, but intense.

He likes what he hears. It has the ring of a substantial piece of the investigative puzzle falling onto his desk.

'It's a wristband. A clump of bands, actually.'

'You recognize them?'

'I think I might. Not positive. A lot of guys wear wristbands these days. Leather and beads. It's a thing.'

'But there's something about these?'

'About one of them. The focus is off, but I think it has a single embossed metal bead. Attached to braided strands of black leather . . . I think. Hard to be certain.'

'I can have the tech guys at headquarters work on it.'

'There's something you should know.' Because if he doesn't, then the wristband in question and its owner just might be on a flight to Toronto and subsequently into the untraceable bowels of mainland Canada.

'I'm listening.'

'One of my clients wears wristbands.'

He's expecting more.

'One of which has a single embossed metal bead.'

'You're certain?'

'I've noticed it.'

'What's embossed on it?'

'I didn't pay it that much attention.'

'And his name, Mr. Synard?'

'Marco Tolentino. From Markham, Ontario.'

'Sounds Italian.'

'Filipino.'

'Was he in any way connected to Amanda Thomsen?'

'In the same way we all were. We were all staying at the same B & B. We all had breakfast together.'

He hears something in my voice. He senses there's more. Which, of course, there is. And which will undoubtedly throw a bombshell into the timeline to get us to the ferry on schedule and on to Deer Lake.

'Continue.'

The choice I have is to tell what I observed, openly, minus speculation. Or remain on mute. And down the road have the shit hit the proverbial fan.

And with it face possible obstruction of justice. There is no choice.

I disclose to Larsen what I observed, from the carefully en-gineered foreplay around the fire to the potential for something coming to a climax behind closed doors, to the cryptic, flaccid exchange over breakfast. I try not to be judgmental.

Larsen's note-taking is intermittent, somewhat ham-fisted. He's having trouble capturing it all. When I pause, he eventu-ally stops and looks across the desk at me. He's unsatisfied, but hesitant to say so.

'I get it,' he says, demonstrating a need to retake the lead.

'This is the key question. To which you are to provide as clear an answer as possible.'

Am I about to argue with that? No. Besides which I, as much as anyone, am seeking the truth about what happened to Amanda Thomsen.

'Did Marco Tolentino have an opportunity to make his way to the lighthouse in Point Amour, on his own, while Amanda Thomsen was there?'

I take my time. 'He took our vehicle to Blanc Sablon to pick up a bottle of wine. Other than that, he was with the rest of us in Forteau. Point Amour, as we both know, is in the opposite direction. He wouldn't have had time to go to both places. He was away from the B & B just over an hour. I was keeping track because we had a dinner reservation at the Florian. I remember he left at about 5:45. He got back just before seven.'

The corporal likes precise timelines. I'm back in his good books.

'How can you be sure he went to Blanc Sablon?'

'He came back with a bottle of sparkling wine.'

'What makes you think he didn't already have one in his possession?'

'He went out the door empty-handed.'

'There's a liquor outlet in L'Anse-au-Loup. Not far past the turnoff to Point Amour.'

I wasn't aware of that. In any case, what is he implying? That Marco lied, picked up a bottle there, then headed to the lighthouse. I very much doubt it. But I will hand it to the young man. He's not about to leave any stone, no matter how far-fetched, unturned.

'Do you know the name of the wine?'

As a matter of fact, I do.

He's on his phone. 'Hello, Mr. Normore. Corporal Larsen here.' There's a pause. 'Yes, very unfortunate. That's all I can say at this point.' Another pause. 'I'm calling to ask if you would you check your liquor inventory. I need to know if you carry a sparkling wine called . . . just a minute.' He looks over at me, holding the phone away from him. 'How do you pronounce that first word again?'

'Cuvée.'

He turns back to the phone. 'Cuvée Catharine.'

While he waits, Larsen informs me, 'They sell snowmobiles, ATVs, chainsaws. They have a gas bar and the Liquor Express dealership for this part of the coast.'

Entrepreneurial, to say the least. 'One-stop shopping for the b'ys heading to their cabins for the weekend.'

Larsen doesn't crack a smile. I thought it deserved one.

I add, 'Doubt if the b'ys are into Cuvée Catharine.'

As it turns out, someone is. Mr. Normore is back on the phone. 'Very good. Not a big seller I take it?' Once the corporal has parted ways with Mr. Normore, he turns back to me. 'I was wrong. A steady demand apparently. The b'ys, as you put it, think it makes a good choice for anniversary overnights at the cabin.'

The wine-buying habits of southern Labrador aside, Larsen has made a point. Which he now takes a step further. He calls in Corporal Beauchamp and gets him to call the SAQ and any other outlets that sell wine in Blanc Sablon to check their inventory for a certain cuvée. Pronounced rather well, I will add. The eager, bilingual corporal is on it right away.

In the meantime, there is the matter of my statement. I have it in hand, on a USB stick. Larsen does the honours and soon it is spit out of the detachment's printer. On official RCMP letterhead, it has taken on extra credibility. I read it through, correct and initial a typo, then sign and date it.

Beauchamp returns to the office. He's not sure if the results of his phone calls are what Larsen is hoping for, but it's conclusive. 'Nobody's heard of it.'

It's what Corporal Larsen was hoping for all right. He's suddenly very much in the driver's seat.

As for me, I appear to be along for the ride.

Beauchamp is not done yet. 'While I was waiting on them to check their inventories I did a search online,' he says. Eagerness beyond the call of duty. 'Cuvée Catharine might sound French, but it's actually made in Ontario.'

I shrink deeper into the passenger seat.

Larsen sits even further upright. 'I need to talk to Marco Tolentino straight away. And, as a matter of fact, the others in your group as well. Nobody's going anywhere until I'm finished with them.'

I saw it coming. Deep breath. Okay, no point in being pissed off.

Make it severely peeved. The one o'clock ferry crossing is out the window. What the frig happens to the tour agenda now?

'No need to interview my teenage son.'

'I'm afraid so.'

'How about the friggin' dog? He's always been very observant.'

A slip of the tongue, the provisional f-word. Larsen is not amused. Beauchamp holds back a smile in deference to his superior. Confirms my theory. You can pick out a dog lover every time. They have a heightened sense of humour.

Okay, let's get this straight. Granted, Marco's story doesn't entirely add up. The least he has done is lie about his run for the now-infamous bottle of wine. So it's likely he dodged over to the Liquor Express in L'Anse-au-Loup. Say he then took the side road into Point Amour. Say he somehow (we don't know how) got inside the lighthouse. Either the entrance was left unlocked (which I doubt) or Amanda let him in (which I also doubt, given her aloofness toward him over breakfast). Which leaves the bead-and-leather wristband.

Still fuzzy in the photo. Say it was his wrist. Say he was on the catwalk with Amanda. That doesn't add up either. And even if it was him, who's to say it was any more than an encounter (amicable or otherwise), after which Amanda saw him out the door, and he left and drove back to the B & B in Forteau?

Larsen has his sights set on a scenario in which Marco pushed Amanda over the railing before hightailing it down the one-hundred-plus steps and making a quick exit from the lighthouse. Which leaves a pile of unanswered questions. Why was the door locked when I arrived? Who locked it? Would Amanda have handed him over the key before he turned on her? (Not likely.) Would he have had the strength to subdue her while searching her pockets for the key, before then tossing her over the railing? (Even less likely considering how agile Amanda looked to be.)

I keep the questions to myself. At this point it's better if Larsen comes up with them on his own. I long ago concluded that cops prefer to reach their own conclusions, without suggestions from civilians who might just be working with a bit more grey matter. They like the control.

The questions will emerge in due course. Once the corporal has Marco behind closed doors, his miscalculations are bound to raise their emphatic head.

In the meantime, I have no choice but rebook to a later ferry crossing and hope we make it, with the prospect of then driving the three-and-a-half hours to Deer Lake, arriving late at night, yet still in time for the pharos four to catch their flight in the morning.

Corporal Larsen and Corporal Beauchamp are gearing up. They don bulletproof vests—overkill, to my mind, but that's also best kept to myself—the word POLICE blazoned across the front of them. Sidearms are in close proximity. A peaked cap with the distinctive yellow band and crest covers Larsen's receding hairline, while Beauchamp opts for the more youthful but still official ball cap. There's no mistaking their status. They mean business.

The police cruiser precedes me to the Grenfell B & B. We park side by side, but the Durango quickly shrinks to second place. The cruiser's emphatic band of red, yellow and blue stripes, in combination with the eager-to-flare light bar, demand undivided attention. Though rather lifeless, even the RCMP emblem with its ritzy royal crown atop an amputated buffalo head surrounded by a wreath of maple leaves can instill dread in the average, law-abiding Joe.

I suspect at least one person inside has caught sight of our arrival. Word would have spread to the breakfast table and beyond. No surprise then that Peggy has the front door open before we reach the steps of the entrance.

'Gentlemen.' She struggles for more, but the bulletproof vests leave her bereft of speech.

Corporal Larsen steps smartly into his role. 'We would like to speak to your guests, those in Mr. Synard's tour group.'

'All my guests are in that group . . .' She needs a moment, having brought to mind the former guest that wasn't. 'Two are still eat . . . I'll inform them . . . all of them.'

'Is there someplace where we can assemble?' There is. 'Is there a second entrance to the B & B?' There is, off the kitchen. 'Lock it and then proceed to inform your guests.'

Larsen and Beauchamp stand side by side, bulking up to extend themselves the full width of the hallway—a mental barrier to any guest who might dispute the seriousness of the situation, a physical barrier to any one of them who might be half-witted enough to consider making a getaway. Again, to my mind, overkill.

The sitting room fills to capacity. Its door is closed. Larsen and Beauchamp have routed a herd of six males, all intimidated, although to varying degrees.

It's only appropriate that I step forward and set the stage. 'Let me introduce Corporal Larsen and Corporal Beauchamp of the Forteau detachment of the Royal Canadian Mounted Police. As I have previously informed you, an investigation is underway into the unexpected death of Amanda Thomsen, whose acquaintance we all made during the brief time she resided at the Grenfell B & B. As you will appreciate, it is the duty of the RCMP to interview any member of the public who has been in recent contact with the deceased. Therefore—'

'Thank you, Mr. Synard. I'll take it from here.'

I thought I was doing rather well. It goes to show the limited capacity of Mounties to be less than the centre of attention. Too long in red serge uniforms sitting atop faultlessly trained horses.

'We will now proceed, bearing in mind you are all to re-main in the building until called to this room.'

He names each of them, drawn from my official statement of course. Marco is noticeably the last on the list. Gaffer, I regret to say, didn't make it.

'Return to your room or take a seat in the dining room, whichever you choose.'

Andy's hand is in the air, rather like that of a schoolboy. Although he is trying not to show it, Larsen must be pleased to see them fall in line so quickly. He acknowledges Andy with a curt, 'Yes?'

'How long do you expect this will take? I really don't want to miss our ferry connection. My wife is expecting me in BC tomorrow. It's our anniversary. We've been married thirty-five years.'

Inwardly, I smile. Larsen is unprepared for personal trivia. He struggles to retain the assertive atmosphere he has set in place. 'I can only say it will take as long as it needs to take.'

Now I know the derivation of the word copout.

Andy, either dissatisfied or confused, raises his hand a second time, at which point Larsen inserts, 'I'll let Mr. Synard deal with matters of ferry schedules. Thank you in advance for your cooperation. We will begin the first interview in five minutes. Please vacate this room until you are called.'

I have a role after all. That was good of the corporal—to reinstate me, even if it was rather convenient to do so.

I face Andy's same question, now awaiting me outside. I assure them all that even though the one o'clock crossing is no longer part of the game plan, we'll be in plenty of time for the six o'clock run, after which we're home free and it's on to Deer Lake.

'Supper's on me once we board the ferry.'

It does nothing to calm the waters. It's turned into a costly impulse that now pisses me off.

'In the meantime, what do we do for lunch?' asks Andy. 'We can't leave the building.' The man's gut is never far from his mind.

Peggy, who all this time has been waiting for someone to emerge from the sitting room, has overheard our exchange. She comes to the rescue. 'I can put on a pot of soup. And make some sandwiches.' The dear woman.

They disperse, at varying speeds. Marco, noticeably, heads directly to his room, shutting the door firmly behind him.

Peggy hangs close to me, expecting some indication of what transpired behind closed doors. 'Your sitting room is soon to become the scene of a fact-finding expedition. If I were you, I'd be charging rent.' Only half in jest.

She searches for a compatible response. 'Think I should offer them coffee?'

'I wouldn't if I were you. They're fired up enough as it is. You'd only be adding fuel. But I'll have one, if you wouldn't mind.'

She wanders off to the kitchen to put on a fresh brew and to start rounding up ingredients for the pot of soup.

'So,' says Nick, who approaches me, dog leash in hand, 'what do we do about Gaffer? He needs to do his business.'

Gaffer has not fared well over the past day. Not enough human time, not enough exercise. He needs an extended walk, a chance to socialize with the wider world.

At that moment, the officious voice of Corporal Beauchamp is infiltrating the hallway. Nick has been summoned. It appears that Larsen is starting with the person of only marginal interest and working his way up.

Nick is no longer intimidated. I think he's now viewing this as a life experience to add to a resumé. He hands me the leash. 'He's desperate.' Referring to the dog.

My solution to the Gaffer situation is to borrow the thin but sturdy piece of nylon rope that Peggy has fortunately uncovered in a bottom kitchen drawer, use it to extend the dog leash, and then convince Peggy it's okay to unlock the side entrance, so I can stand outside while Gaffer roams, sniffs, and eventually expels. My intention is to break Larsen's directive only long enough to fill the doggie bag. I assume I'll be forgiven.

This all takes time. But before I re-enter the detention centre, Nick reappears.

'That went well,' he says, looking very pleased with himself. 'Not that I had a great deal to offer.'

Still, rack it up as yet another experience resulting from investigative time spent with his father. 'I'd avoid telling your mother if I were you.'

A wink and a nod from the lad. He then proceeds to relate the line of questioning.

'They, of course, wanted to know everything that happened from the first time I set eyes on her up to and including that last time, looking up from the base of the lighthouse. Straight-forward. No kinks in the narrative as far as that goes.'

Of course, Nick had relatively little contact. He has none of the behind-the-scenes-suspicions that I have. It's best kept that way.

'I did tell them she could be odd at times. You know—the sexual innuendo at breakfast.'

A bit of a double take on my part. Now he's talking "sexual innuendo" to the cops?

'Amanda was a bit out there,' he says. 'Right?'

'I don't want to be judgmental.'

'That's not like you, Dad.'

I let that pass. 'I'm thinking it's okay to take Gaffer for a walk now that the officers have finished with you.'

'Amanda had some hang-ups. But, like I said before, I don't think it was suicide.'

He's not about to be redirected. He waits me out.

'You said this to the cops?'

'Of course not. I presented my observations. I let them draw their own conclusions.'

What is this? He's put everything in some kind of perspective. He took a course in IB on critical thinking and embraced it with a vengeance? He's grown up intellectually before my eyes and I missed it?

Plus the fact that the cops will now have seen a serious gap in my official statement, i.e., the "sexual innuendo."

I hand him the leash, minus the rope extension.

Accepted, but not before a parting comment. 'I feel sorry for her. Counselling would have helped, I think.'

He's likely right. Unfortunately, I've been forced to deal with what happened, not what could have been.

It is now a series of zero hours for the pharos four, beginning with Andy. I suspect the questioners prefer to get the most talkative and potentially irksome out of the way first. Understandable.

Andy is followed by Calvin, then André. Marco is the closing act. When he is called, I make a point of observing from a distance. He has reworked his appearance by shaving the calculated stubble that normally covered the lower half of his face, in addition to replacing the "Keep Calm and Carry On Running" sweatshirt that he wore at breakfast. Smart choices. Though I doubt it will have much impact, given that the early morning first impression has already been embedded in RCMP minds.

While Marco is behind closed doors with police officers having a go at their primary person of interest, the remainder of the tour group has gathered in the dining room to debrief over coffee. The lads are tense.

'We can't possibly be suspects,' says Calvin decisively.

'These interviews are regular police procedure.' Downplaying is good at this point. What we don't want is unnecessary panic in the ranks.

'I have a knot in my stomach about this,' says Andy. 'My stomach is uncertain at the best of times.'

'And Pepto-Bismol is of no help?' Injection of wit—also a calculated strategy.

Nick is the only one chuckling. He cuts it short, realizing he's out of sync with the general mood.

Even André, who normally can be counted on to at least smile, is deadpan. The man, I've noticed, is particularly cheerless around police officers. I suspect there've been encounters in the past that have not gone well.

'Cops can be assholes,' he announces, under his breath, but loud enough to be heard around the table.

What did I say? Whatever his perspective, it is absolutely not in our best interest to be anything but courteous with Corporals Larsen and Beauchamp. 'Hold your fire, André. We need to get through this and get to the ferry. On time.'

He peers at me indulgently. 'No one is going to lose their cool, Sebastian.'

Deep breath, Sebastian. Deep breath.

If nothing else, we're all on the same page.

Suddenly even that consolation disintegrates.

'You're kidding me! I'm calling a fuckin' lawyer.' Easily penetrates the closed door. Marco has lost his cool.

We freeze in position, primed to hang on every word.

There are no more, at least none loud enough for us to hear. We wait, glancing at each other, in silence, except for the sudden, discordant sounds of Peggy stirring soup.

The sitting room door opens.

'Sebastian.' It's Larsen, his one word stiff and uncompromising. I'm jerked away from the table. Not promising.

'Your client is being detained for further questioning at the detachment.'

Another monkey wrench crashing into our already readjusted plans. 'For how long?'

'That remains to be seen. An additional investigating officer is flying in from St. John's.'

Larsen's contact with his superiors has triggered deployment of the heavyweights. Forensics, of course, for the crime scene. And someone specially trained in interrogation, whose first job will now be to grill the agitated Marco.

'What about the others on the tour?'

'They're free to go. I have all their contact information should we need it. The inspector will want to talk to you. That can wait until tomorrow, if need be.'

'Once the others board their flight in Deer Lake, I hadn't

planned on coming back to Forteau.'

'It's obvious your plans will have to change, Mr. Synard.'

No need for the condescension. 'This is a criminal investigation,' he adds unnecessarily. 'The law requires your cooperation.'

I'm fully aware of what the law requires. 'I'd like a word with Marco before you take him to the detachment.'

He hesitates, but in the end agrees, with a caution. 'You will note that anything he says to you in any way related to the investigation must be fully disclosed. You are not his lawyer. There is no attorney-client privilege.'

That, also, I'm fully aware of. I enter the sitting room. The two officers remove themselves, as if they are doing me a favour. I close the door behind them.

Marco is bent over, elbows on his knees, head in his hands. I sit in an armchair across from him.

'Get me a lawyer, Sebastian. I'm not sayin' another fuckin' thing to them until I talk to a lawyer.'

'Cool it, Marco. Calm down.'

That said, how do I deal with this? The guy could be guilty as hell, in which case I still see no point in getting involved. Let the cops handle it.

Then again, I have some responsibility in the situation. At this point, he's still part of the tour. The least I can do is help him find a lawyer. After that he's on his own.

'No lawyers in Forteau for sure. I doubt if there are any in southern Labrador. Not enough population.'

I take out my phone. I search for the website of the Law Society of Newfoundland and Labrador. Connect to its membership directory. Just as I suspected. No one close.

'The closest lawyer is in St. Anthony. Depending on the ferry, you're talking four hours for him to get here. Minimum.' I write down the phone number, tear the page from my notebook and hand it to him. 'When you get to the detachment, call him. His name is Colin Baxter. He'll advise you over the phone.'

'Sebastian, man, I need all the help I can get. You're more than a tour guide, you're a private investigator. Anyone who googles your name knows that.'

Apparently so. I shouldn't be surprised.

'You got to help me.'

I don't *have* to do anything. Marco got himself into this mess, he's the one to get himself out. Time to face it—I'm talking to a suspect. Possibly a murderer.

'I have to get back to the island. The others have to catch their flight in Deer Lake.'

'I didn't do it. I didn't fuckin' do it. I didn't push Amanda Thomsen over that railing. You got to believe me.'

I stand up. 'It makes no difference what I believe. You get that lawyer. He's the guy to help you.'

'Sebastian, you know me, you know all that happened. I'll hire you, too. Whatever it costs, I got the money.'

We're standing face to face. 'Marco, I can't help you.'

'Can't or fuckin' won't?'

I step past him to the door. 'You're on your own, Marco. Spend your money on a lawyer.'

I close the door behind me. Through it, a very loud, 'Fuck!'

That's it. Out of my hands. Before Larsen asks, I tell him. 'I gave him contact information for a lawyer. That's all I did.'

He doesn't take it any further. I retreat to my room. I have no intention of being around when they escort Marco to the cop car.

I pack away the rest of my clothes, zipper the suitcase, and sit on the edge of the unmade bed until I'm sure they're gone. Nick, returning with Gaffer, confirms it.

I'm determined to put all this shit out of my head, get on

with the remainder of the day, and get to the ferry. The quicker I see the goddamn road the better.

I take to the dining room and try to calm down. The group that's now the pharos three is rabid to know the reason for the outburst from Marco and what was a dramatic exit of their former travel companion to the cop station.

'He's on the RCMP radar as someone who may have had more contact than the rest of us with Amanda Thomsen.' Downplaying is still the option.

No longer a tenable one.

'C'mon, Sebastian,' says André. 'Play straight with us. We're not stupid. We all know you're a *détective privé* when you're not a tour guide.'

You, too? How good of Google to up everyone's expectations.

I hesitate. I seethe. I finally open my mouth. 'It would appear Marco and Amanda have been screwing around at some point.'

I anticipate shock. What I get is resignation, tinged with scorn.

'Miscalculation, this time around,' says Calvin.

'His lust for life got the better of him,' says André.

'Doesn't pay to be horny so much of the time,' adds the unambiguous Andy, not without a hint of envy.

Nick is wide-eyed. Horniness, sexual innuendo—they both had their parts to play.

The fellows shed more light on the situation. Apparently Marco, during their stay at the Jag Hotel in St. John's, made a number of forays to the nearby bars of George Street and returned on each occasion with a different young woman willing to share his accommodation for the night.

'He also went looking in Bonavista,' André relates, 'but came back empty-handed.'

'And Twillingate,' adds Calvin. 'Or so he said.'

It appears Marco made no secret of his exploits, except from me and Nick. For whatever reason, he didn't want to mix my business with his pleasure. I'm glad I didn't know.

'I assume that, once they talk to him further, they'll release him in time to catch the ferry?' André is expecting an answer from me.

'That remains to be seen, I guess.' Actually, I don't guess. Marco is in a lot more shit than I'm about to disclose. That part is very much under wraps to all but the RCMP and its tight-lipped informant.

Peggy appears, shell-shocked by what she must have over-heard. She is holding a much-appreciated change of focus in the form of a tureen of steaming vegetable soup and, with a second speechless appearance, a platter of thick roast beef sandwiches topped with hefty half-slices of dill pickles.

They help turn our attention to what we can do to kill the couple of hours before we'll be heading to the ferry terminal, with or without Marco.

'Lighthouses,' garbles Andy, wallowing in the thickness of Peggy's homemade bread.

Absolutely not.

The remainder of the bite finally makes it down his gullet. 'Any more close by? Even if they're not special in any way.'

'Even if, as we like to say, they're *not up to much*.' Calvin pauses. A rare smile.

Yes, Calvin, I get it. And it's not particularly funny. But I have to say that, under the circumstances, I do appreciate the effort.

André sets aside his soup spoon. He's into his phone. It's not long before the intense searching results in a self-satisfied smile. 'Lighthousefriends.com tells me there's one just over the Quebec border.' His enthusiasm rises, as does his voice. '*Phare de l'Île Greenly.* And get this—in 1928 the *Bremen*, a German Junkers W 33, left Ireland for New York on what was to be the first non-stop, east–west flight across the Atlantic, but was forced down because of an oil leak. Thirty-six-and-a-half hours after takeoff, the plane landed on the ice of a small pond near Île Greenly Lighthouse.'

Playing on my gluttony for historical detail, André thinks he's done a good job of sucking me in.

Sorry. Like I wasn't on Lighthousefriends.com for hours on end researching lighthouses in preparation for this tour. Like I didn't check out Quebec lighthouses near the border of southern Labrador.

'Unfortunately,' I tell him, 'Île Greenly takes twenty minutes to reach by boat from Blanc Sablon. It might be a bit of a strain on your eyes to see it from shore.'

'You could be right,' says André reluctantly. A pause while he checks a couple more websites.

I return to my soup.

Calvin, it seems, is not put off by André's cut of humble pie. 'There's a lighthouse on an island off West St. Modeste, across a channel of, if I remember correctly, ninety metres, which means there should be a good view of it, even if we don't find anyone with a boat willing to take us across.'

'*Was* a lighthouse,' I counter. 'It was decommissioned more than a decade ago. Likely in a state of disrepair. Who wants to end the tour by gazing at a defunct lighthouse soon to fall to the ground?'

Evidently they all do.

'We came to see lighthouses,' says Calvin. 'We don't like to discriminate. They all have a history, even if at the present point in time they're not up to much.' He pauses, in the hope that I might at least smile this time. When I don't, he continues, with added intensity, 'Lighthouses are like people.

They appreciate it when someone recognizes their neglect. Each lighthouse in its own way is a survivor.'

Cry me a river. How about he adopts one and takes it home?

I *was* about to suggest a hike on one of southern Labrador's several exceptional trails. I *was* thinking it would be a prime opportunity to really unwind and rid ourselves of all that tension. I reconsider.

Not that it needs repeating, but these guys are obsessed. They long ago used up their stockpile of reality checks. They'll be on their deathbeds yearning to be at the top of the highest lighthouse in the world, believing it will shorten their journey to the Promised Land.

Our view from the wharf at West St. Modeste, across the water to St. Modeste Island, is nothing if not bleak. The runt of a wooden lighthouse looks ready, willing, and able to give up the ghost. Paint deeply scarred by wind and weather, door hinges now clumps of rust, the slumping catwalk clinging on for dear life—very sad to think it would be our final lighthouse image of the tour.

Contrary to Calvin's manifesto, I detect limited empathy from the other two. And, I suspect, potential agreement with my unvoiced assessment.

As we are standing there, we're approached from behind by an older man. He's quick to engage with strangers, curious as to what we're about. I'd say he's lived here all his life, part of the bedrock of this Labrador community.

'Havin' a look, are ya b'ys? Bit of an eyesore now, but she brought a lot of comfort in her day.'

The lads latch on immediately. 'The lighthouse—she was a going concern?' asks Calvin.

'Yes, sir. Red flash every three seconds. Foghorn when we

needed it, every twenty seconds.'

'She more than paid her way?' Another prompt.

'She was a survivor, sir. But now the heart is gone out of her.'

Music to Calvin's ears. 'I feel the pain.'

'Would you fellers like to have a closer look? Climb aboard the boat and we'll take a dart over.' Lots of time on his hands, and apparently nothing he likes better than a change of pace in his day.

'My name is Cecil, by the way.' He extends a thick, work-toughened hand to each of us.

I pull out my phone and grab a quick look at the screen. There's no argument to be made that we don't have the time to be doing this.

In any case, the pharos three, Calvin in the lead, are already making their way to where the boat is tied up. Nick is not far behind.

'Cecil probably doesn't have enough life jackets,' I caution.

In one ear and out the other. The implication being it will take all of three minutes to cross the channel on a day when there's no wind and no chance of falling overboard. Not something, however, that aligns with a tour guide's insurance policy.

But the fact is Cecil does have enough life jackets, with what he retrieves from the storage box of his own boat and that of his son's boat tied up next to his. Only Gaffer is left out. But, as Nick reminds me, the mutt is capable of a very efficient dog paddle.

There's no reason, then, to be anything but charmed that Cecil has us all aboard, his sure hand on the tiller of his outboard, his contented face catching the sun. I think we've made his day.

Not only that, but Cecil drops a lump of information that jolts me free of what misgivings remain. 'You knows about the young woman who fell off the lighthouse in Point Amour?' he shouts to me above the noise of the outboard. 'She was sittin' where you're sittin' now. Two days ago. I brought her over to the lighthouse just like I'm doin' with you today. Over and back again, her and the feller what was with her.'

I'm dumbstruck for the moment. Then I realize I shouldn't be. It would only make sense that it would be one of the lighthouses she photographed. Inactive and decrepit, but photogenic. All part of what she'd been hired to do.

'That would have been the same day she checked into the Grenfell B & B,' I tell Cecil, 'where we also were staying.' The questions I have for Cecil will have to wait until we are ashore on the island.

With the exception of the less-than-agile Andy, we manage to do so without getting our feet wet. The boat secured, Cecil leads the short trek over the shoreline rocks and through patches of long grass. I claim his attention. 'The young woman who died, her name was Amanda. Did it look like she had a lot on her mind when she was here? Did she appear to be upset about anything?'

'Not for me to see. She was all about takin' pictures, but that's nothin' strange. When she was done, we got to talkin'. Turns out her mother's people were Buckles from L'Anse-au-Diable.'

The lads could be forgiven for their vacant looks, but Buckle is not an uncommon surname in Labrador. And as for L'Anse-au-Diable, once past the oral corruption of the French *diable*, I recall it was a small community along the coast that no longer exists. The name translates into Devil's Cove—very apt, apparently.

'In the 1960s, the people got fed up with being cut off from we fellers in West St. Modeste during the winter months,' Cecil tells us. 'So they shut 'er down and moved. Her mother would have been a baby at the time. The family settled in Forteau, from what she told me. Her mother grew up and went off to university, got married and ended up selling houses. Imagine, little Asti Buckle from L'Anse-au-Diable one of the top real estate agents in St. John's.'

I can't quite. But I have more pressing things on my mind. While the lads take in the lighthouse in all its abandoned glory, I'm extracting whatever information I can from Cecil. 'Who was the guy with her? Another photographer?'

'No, b'y, never had a camera. From the time we got aboard the boat, he was looking all around and scribbling down stuff in a notebook. I asked him what he was at. Observations, he said, for a project. From what I could tell she was taking the pictures and he was doing the writing up, for some kinda book.'

'A bit odd, was he?'

'You could say that. He was a tall bugger. Six foot four if he was an inch. Built like a brick shithouse, and poor as Job's turkey.'

Dare I ask. 'What do you mean?'

'Knees out of he's jeans, a head of blond hair that hadn't seen a comb in weeks. Old plaid shirt with the buttons missing—showing off he's gut muscles if you ask me.'

I get the picture. Nick, standing nearby, is amused. Maybe even envious. The kid works out sometimes, but he doesn't have the obsession that would get him a six-pack.

Cecil is not exactly tuned to current youth culture. 'Doesn't spend much time on TikTok,' Nick says, chuckling, when Cecil's attention has turned to the others as they get up close and personal with the lighthouse.

'Did you get the fellow's name?' I ask Cecil when he turns back.

'The girl called him Babe.'

Nick is having trouble containing his grin.

The pharos three circle the lighthouse with resolute interest, despite its neglect. If they are to believe that what's before them once played a pivotal role in the history of this coast, their imaginations will have to shift into high gear.

Cecil is of considerable help in that department. 'You've heard of Yankee privateers,' he says. 'Well, b'ys, they was here in droves.'

What he doesn't say is the American Revolutionary War (during which said privateers were out and about) predates the lighthouse by at least a hundred and fifty years. In all likelihood two, if not three, of the pharos realize this, but choose to ignore it.

'No kidding,' says André.

'Good to know,' says Calvin. 'It puts it in perspective.'

Which amounts to accepting that the American Revolution laid the groundwork for the eventual construction of the lighthouse, something which would certainly put it in a class by itself.

'What sights it once saw,' says Andy. 'If only this lightship could speak.'

Yes, Andy, if only.

Our afternoon has passed. Back at Grenfell B & B I get in touch with Larsen at the Forteau detachment. Not good. The inspector from St. John's has yet to arrive. Marco won't be going anywhere.

Larsen is short on detail, anxious to get back to a situation that has overwhelmed his two-man detachment. What I tell him about Cecil's encounter with Amanda and "Babe" is a further complication. The last thing he needs.

'Thanks for letting me know,' he says, blandly. The intake of air is audible.

'I'll see you tomorrow.'

'Yes. Tomorrow. That's it for now. I have to go.' A negligible pause. End of call.

Within a half-hour, we set off for the ferry. I would say Peggy has no regrets about seeing us go. I, however, will be back tomorrow. The unwanted drama in her life will continue.

The Durango seat formerly occupied by Marco stirs mixed emotions. Remorse on the one hand, relief on the other. I have little choice but to explain why Marco remains in the hands of the Mounties, forcing his former lighthouse colleagues to wrap their heads around the fact that we might all have been sharing the vehicle with a murderer.

'His sexual forays got the better of him.' That would be Calvin, quick to commit to what is in his mind a rock-solid position.

'He had an appetite he couldn't control.' Which I might have found humorous, coming as it does from Andy, had the situation not been so grim.

André, on the other hand, has sympathy for the fellow. 'If she was pushed to her death, I doubt if it was Marco. There's a huge gap between craving it and killing someone if she didn't play the game.'

Of all of us, I'd say André has had the most experience with someone who did or did not "play the game." His comment hangs in the air. I'm not about to go there.

The fact is the three of them are withdrawing from the scene. They'll soon be flying off to places very far removed from whatever is about to transpire in the police station in Forteau. By tomorrow, their mainland selves will be back in motion and they will each have a dozen other concerns taking over their lives.

As for Nick, he'll be boarding the bus back to St. John's. He's got the job waiting for him. And Gaffer? The mutt has no choice but to stick with me.

Or, I should say, with me and Mae, who arrives tomorrow morning. A dog wasn't in the original getaway plan, but there it is. He's a reasonable pup. He'll respect our private space.

Once we get to that private space. Once I've done my bit with RCMP. I texted Mae to give her a heads-up on a slight change in plans. I avoided relating the incident at Point Amour. She'd only worry. By the end of tomorrow, all that will be behind us and we'll be slipping into our post-tour, getaway state of play. My imagination swells at the thought.

For now, downplaying continues to be my go-to strategy. As I said to Mae, it will be but a brief "diversion" to Forteau, and by Sunday we'll be back on track, soaking up the flavours of Conche and the French Shore, on the northeastern tip of the Great Northern Peninsula of Newfoundland.

As the MV *Qajaq W* departs Blanc Sablon, we're on deck, scanning the receding coast of Labrador. That would be the Île Greenly lighthouse, the one I deftly avoided pursuing earlier this afternoon.

And for very good reason, as is now confirmed. It is nothing more than a skeletal steel tower. Serves its purpose but it's sure as heck nothing to get their pharologist genes excited.

It can, nevertheless, legitimately be added to their checklist. Seen and somewhat experienced, if not actually rubbed up against. André has his binoculars fixed on the raw-boned lighthouse, hoping for something more. Eventually he lets them fall back against his chest, resigned to the obvious. He can't argue when the real thing is even less impressive than the picture he called up on his iPhone. Touching, really. He tried.

This is not going out on the high note I had intended.

Yet, if my memory serves me well, there is a remedy. And a dramatically good one at that. (Dramatically, at least, in the eyes of pharologists.)

Once we've had the free-for-all supper, completed the

crossing, and are about to head down the peninsula to Deer Lake, I make a short, unscheduled detour—a twenty-minute run to Flower's Cove and a view of its retired but delightfully distinctive lighthouse.

It, too, is on an island and it, too, we view from across a body of water. But there the similarity between it and our most recent encounters ends.

'A lighthouse in the fullest sense of the word,' I note unabashedly. 'And the only one of its kind in all of Newfoundland and Labrador.'

The keeper's dwelling house and the rectangular fifteen-metre tower with its lantern room were built as a single wooden structure. Painted white, trimmed in red, and looking for all the world like a house with an observatory atop one corner. Looking cared for despite the fact it ceased operation more than fifty years ago. The lads can't help but be impressed.

Albeit, in the case of André, reluctantly. There is a fix for that. 'Le phare,' I tell him, 'was built and paid for, not by Newfoundland, but by Canada, to service the steamships that passed through the Strait of Belle Isle, heading to Québec City and Montreal.'

His ears are noticeably erect. Yet he says, 'Pas de surprise.'

How about this, then? 'The lighthouse was operated by the Lavallee family from Quebec for almost the entire time it was in operation.'

His sense of provincial patriotism cannot withstand the pressure. 'Shit. Pour de vrai?' he says. 'If that doesn't take the fuckin' cake. C'est malade!'

Got to love that about André—his bilingual dexterity. It's definitely the high note I was aiming for.

With that, it's back in the Durango, sights refocused on Deer Lake.

It will take us four hours. Conversation dies away. Daylight eventually fades and with it any remnant of camaraderie. Unavoidably perhaps, the vacuum is filled with mixed emotions. Low-level humming would seem to indicate a suppressed urge for optimism. But it fights to find a balance with thoughts of Marco abandoned to what by now must be a band of hard-nosed cops. My passengers have either sunk into their own emotions or drifted off to sleep.

By the time the dashboard clock reaches midnight, with a half-hour still to drive, the vehicle resounds with a low-grade but distinct rumble of snoring. Reassuring in its own right.

It's the soundtrack all the way to the parking lot of the Deer Lake Motel, transitioning to drowsy mutter upon exiting the vehicle, then a lethargic check-in. And eventually, for the tour leader, a peaty dram. The last full day of *Right On! Light On!* has, thankfully, ended.

SHINE A LIGHT

IT'S A FOND farewell. Delighted they came.

Equally delighted to see them go through security at eight in the morning and into the waiting lounge, before boarding an Air Canada flight that will get André to Montreal, Calvin to Toronto, and Andy (with a connection) to Vancouver. Andy, according to his calculation, has just enough time between flights to squeeze in lunch. A sizable relief.

Yet the tour hasn't truly terminated. Left behind is Marco, the impediment to closing the books and moving on.

A bit callous to call him an impediment. But to be honest, I have a great deal of trouble rousing sympathy for the man. I'll deal with the situation and remain on standby until my input is no longer needed by the RCMP or his lawyer. If Marco is charged and it goes to trial, that could take months or even longer. In the meantime, life marches on.

At this very moment (not long after the lads are out of sight and out of mind), Mae enters the terminal, having deplaned from Provincial Airlines' regular morning flight from St. John's.

The relief and revival are immediate, the wraparound hug prolonged.

'Must have been a tough week,' she says once we've dis-engaged.

'There's a story.'

Which we will get to, but not before she embraces Nick. It does me no end of good to see how well the two of them get along.

'How about we grab a coffee?'

Nick, sensing it's best if I break the news to Mae on my own, is off to take Gaffer for a walk.

The coffee is predictable. Mae's reaction to the story I relate is not.

'Is there a possibility he's innocent?'

It's pretty obvious he's guilty of something, whatever that something might be. I do, however, hold that thought for the time being.

'Always a possibility I suppose.' I'm trying my best to appreciate her perspective. Not easy, given the fact that I've been immersed in the situation and she has not.

'Then you must feel an obligation to pursue it until you're absolutely sure, one way or the other. He's still your client.'

'Technically the tour has ended.'

'But morally you wouldn't want to abandon him.'

A longish pause. 'I agree.'

No need to trigger an argument. I'm doing my best to keep things on an even keel, keep our relationship where it needs to be if this getaway has any chance of garnering the adjective "romantic." I smile affectionately.

And sip my coffee while pointing out that we've loads of time to discuss the whole situation during the drive that's ahead of us. For now, I make a timely change of focus—to Nick. We need to get him to Circle K Convenience, where the DRL bus will be stopping en route to St. John's.

Gaffer proves an additional deflection. Over the months

Mae and I have been together, she and the mutt have bonded quite nicely. In fact, there are times when Gaffer seems to outright prefer her company to mine. I think it's the treats myself, a handful of which she is not long extracting from her tote bag after they reunite.

'He'll be fine,' she tells Nick as we drive off.

'He'll need his exercise,' Nick says to me, a not-so-subtle reference to the fact that he has been on dog-walk duty for most of the tour.

'No worries, pal. When you see him again, he'll be ship-shape and ready to roll.'

I maintain that positive tone right up to the hugs goodbye. Mae and I have to get on the move if we're going to make the three-thirty ferry. Nick has an island-crossing bus ride ahead of him.

'The time will slip by before you know it. You got your phone and junk food?'

'I have *The Iliad* to finish up.'

How about I eat crow and yet again update my perspective on the lad? I forgot—he's getting a head start on the reading list for the start-up of university in a couple of months.

'Yes, do that. Here's a little extra cash. Grab a couple of sandwiches to go with your Homer.'

Mae digs into her tote and retrieves a small box. It appears the tote is a repository for both human and dog treats.

Forest Road Chocolates. Handmade. Locally foraged ingredients. Small batch. I've been a lucky recipient in the past.

'Awesome,' Nick says.

Yes, she's done me one better. Chocolate-coated Homer on a DRL bus. Awesome to say the least.

I hug the lad and wish him well. I'll be honest, nine hours on a bus does have its downsides.

'I'm good,' he says, "Be strong, saith my heart; I am a

soldier; I have seen worse sights than this.'"

He not only reads it, he quotes it. That deserves another hug.

Mae and I hit the road.

'He never ceases to amaze me,' she says. 'You must be quite proud.'

An understatement, of course. I smile broadly. 'Sharp as a bloody tack.'

Leading her directly to, 'What does he think of all this?'

"All this" meaning the Marco situation. 'Hasn't said a big lot.'

'He must have an opinion.' She waits me out.

'He thought Amanda was "odd at times." That she had "some serious hang-ups."'

A straight-out boost to Mae's appetite for more.

So, here we go. An unrestricted, all-encompassing, straight-talking account of what has taken place since Amanda Thomsen stepped out of her sporty green Mini Cooper and approached Grenfell House B & B in Forteau, Labrador.

It consumes less than fifteen minutes, but to my mind I have stopped at nothing.

Mae, not surprisingly, has questions. Shall we say she has a considerable number of them? As gently articulated as they are.

'You still see suicide as the most likely cause of death?'

'I'm on the fence at the moment. I'll admit the picture on her camera was taken at an abnormal angle, suggesting a commotion of some kind.'

'Have you considered the possibility that the person left, and she subsequently jumped of her own free will?'

'I have considered that. Even so, the evidence points to the fact that the person with her was Marco. The RCMP believe that's the trail that has to be followed. I agree.'

'A leather wristband with a bead on it. How common are they?'

'That's debatable.'

My voice is getting a bit edgy. Mae takes a pause. It was starting to sound like an interrogation, something neither of us wants, I'm sure.

Nevertheless, she's not about to stop without posing the key question. She eases into it, as delicately as possible, considering the can of worms that it is. 'If Marco did push her over the railing, what do you think was his motivation?'

She knows I'm always big on motivation; the question has a certain echo-like quality. I pause to pivot to an even more confident role. 'That's yet to be determined. I'm certain the police will discover it in due course.'

She's on the verge of saying more but stops herself.

She feels I'm abandoning Marco. And that's not the Sebastian she knows.

First of all, I'm not abandoning him. I'm letting his situation rest in the hands of the police. And for good cause.

'It's obvious Marco has been up to no good. As the other three have confirmed, he's quick to make his move on women he's only just met. He's been shown to have a temper at times. God knows what went on between him and Amanda the night before, or at the lighthouse. He could very well have some obsessive condition that leads to violent behaviour. I'm sure the RCMP is looking into his background as we speak. They have access to resources that I don't.'

She's hesitating, but in the end, can't hold back. 'That's never stopped you before.'

I say nothing. For the moment.

'This is different.'

She refrains from pressing the point. She knows she's stepped into very sensitive territory. That case on Fogo Island— the woman murdered in a quilt shop—Mae was the one to lead me in directions that helped resolve the case. She knows that, as grateful as I was, I was the decision-maker. I was the one who ultimately reframed the clues to bring the case to its conclusion. I make no bones about it—when I'm the PI, I need my space.

'Have we got time to stop for coffee?' she asks.

We'll make time.

'Two hours to go to the ferry terminal, but I think we're good. There's a restaurant, the Snack Shack, coming up. In the legendary Sally's Cove.'

She thinks I'm being facetious, but I'm not. Far from it.

'Sally's Cove was the site of the pivotal event of the 1971 provincial election.'

It's a welcome diversion. An opportunity for me and something other than speculation and my PI background to step unquestionably into the foreground.

'A very close race, so close that the outcome came down to a recount in the local District of St. Barbe South, where the Tory candidate led by a margin of only eight votes. As it turned out, the hundred and six ballots cast at the polling station in Sally's Cove had been burned after the initial count was complete.'

'Burned?'

'By accident. Bizarre, I know. Nevertheless, no recount was possible. It threw the province into political turmoil that continued for months until finally a new election was called. Yes, Sally's Cove, forever notorious in the annals of Newfoundland history.'

The tidbit makes for a more relaxed coffee, to the point that Mae reaches out to me, so to speak, and covers my hand affectionately with hers. 'This time tomorrow we'll be in Conche. I can't wait.'

There'll be plenty more to take my mind off what's happened once we get to Conche. Mae has planned a couple of things but is leaving it open to whatever activities come our way. If the stroke of her hand is any indication, they could be varied. I, too, can't wait.

We order the Snack Shack's fish and chips (also legendary) for takeout and, following a quick and purposeful jaunt with Gaffer, we're soon back on the road. Mae hand-serves me the moveable feast as I drive.

We've rebonded.

Boarding the MV *Qajaq W* goes like clockwork. I feel good. I feel positive.

In two hours, we'll be in Forteau. I'll spend an hour at the RCMP detachment, two at the most. Another night at the Grenfell B & B, this time with the affectionate Mae. By eight in the morning we'll be back on the ferry, primed for R and R all along the French Shore.

A call to Larsen confirms we'll meet at seven. I make a point of not asking what, if anything, has transpired in my absence. That will become known in time. Yes, I feel level-headed, in control. Come what Mae.

Meanwhile, we make the most of this sunlit, placid crossing. The deck beckons.

Fresh ocean air clears the mind and body of the last remnants of discord. I wrap an arm around Mae's waist and press closer. She reciprocates. The calm after a tempest—undoubtedly the sweetest.

We transition to one of the nearby seating areas. With the ferry now in open waters, the temperature has dropped a few degrees, sending the majority of passengers to the lounges inside. The more adventuresome types remain.

My guess would be most are tourists like ourselves, for whom the approaching Labrador coastline is a novelty. Several have cameras. One fellow is actually looking around, then writing in a notebook. Recording his impressions for posterity.

How nonconformist is that, when most his age are all about smartphones, selfies, and thumbing their way past the real world that surrounds them.

He's been travelling for a while, by the look of the scruffy backpack. Devil-may-care, out to see the world with little money but loads of gumption. Tall, tanned, with a head of sun-bleached hair and torn jeans. When he turns and walks to one of the empty benches, I can see that behind his tight, red, faded T-shirt and open plaid shirt he's built like . . . like a brick . . . shithouse.

Yes, and looks as poor as Job's fucking turkey.

Mae notices my double take. She looks over at the fellow, who's now seated and has gone back to jotting in his notebook. She leans toward my ear.

'You know him?'

I haven't told her about the lighthouse excursion to West St. Modeste. Didn't think it would do anything more than add unnecessary detail.

I tell her now, keeping it to a perfunctory whisper.

'Really?' Intense, yet confined to me alone. My eardrum vibrates with the expectation of detail.

I have none.

'Did you tell the RCMP?'

'Of course.'

Her next line is unspoken, but would be: But you didn't tell me? Let me pre-empt any further question, such as: Didn't you think his connection with the deceased was significant?

'I had no time to be following up. I had to get to Deer Lake and do all the things that had to be done.' Including picking up the person seated next to me. (For the start of what is feeling more and more like a *getaway interruptus*.)

'I see.'

Not exactly an ear-ringing endorsement of my decision-making.

'You have time now.'

Is she suggesting that I wander over to him and casually strike up a conversation? In which I ask if there just happens to be a connection between him and Amanda Thomsen? Is her understanding of investigation procedure that illogical?

Not to put too fine a point on it—yes.

'That's not how it works. It doesn't pay to be overt. There's a better way.' All the time whispering. All the time looking clandestine.

'I see.'

It can only be a matter of time before the follow-up line.

'What might that be?'

There's no denying an opportunity has presented itself to discover something further about what the deceased was up to in the hours previous to showing up at the Grenfell B & B. Whether that's important information is another question. More to the point is whether it's all best left in the hands of the RCMP.

I do, nevertheless, for the sake of the so-called getaway, stand up and walk in the direction of the young man I know by no other name than "Babe."

He looks up as I approach. No trace of a welcoming expression. But neither a trace of a hostile one. He's leadenly neutral.

Except for the T-shirt, which I now see reads "Catch Up With Jesus" and, in smaller print, "Blessed From My Head To-ma-toes." All within the iconic Heinz-shaped ketchup label.

Just what the hell to make of that? I don't know. So I just emit one of the stock local opening lines.

'How's it goin'?'

'This is it.' Which could be taken for cynical, but in Newfoundland it's the standard snappy comeback, although usually said with an element of humour. Not in this case.

I plow ahead. 'I saw you're keen on the landscape. Just thought I'd point out something you might not be aware of. As we're approaching the ferry terminal in Blanc Sablon, look to the left and you'll see a lighthouse.'

'*Phare de l'Île Greenly.*'

Maybe I shouldn't be surprised. At the fact he knows it or at his effortless French.

'What you probably don't know is that the very first east-to-west flight across the Atlantic sprang an oil leak and ended up landing on the ice of a pond just next to the lighthouse. 1928. The *Bremen*, a German Junkers W 33.'

'Awesome.'

The best possible response.

He flicks to a new page of his notebook and jots down a few lines. 'I just might be able to use that. There's more online no doubt.'

Excellent. I'm hoping for him to open up a bit more. As an extended pause continues, I conclude that's not about to happen.

'Thanks,' he says. 'I'll check it out.'

Which leaves me no choice but to hit his emergency response button. 'You know about the Point Amour lighthouse, of course?'

I detect a slight flinch, now turned into a flexing manoeuvre, as if his shoulders are stiff from sitting. The swelling muscles of his upper body expand the T-shirt text. Catch Up With Jesus. A mixed metaphor if I ever saw one.

'Of course,' he says.

'You heard what happened, the young woman falling to her death?'

A pause, stretched to punishing hesitation. 'Yes, I did.'

He knows it's not enough. Further hesitation, still punishing.

'Suicide, apparently,' I add.

'Possibly.' That single word has repercussions. He shuts down the conversation. 'If you'll excuse me, I think I'll grab a coffee.' He stands up.

'It's Sebastian, by the way.' It's nothing he expects or needs to know.

'Jake.'

The automatic response I was aiming for. He leaves the open deck and heads inside.

I wander back to Mae. 'Productive?' she asks as I sit down.

'Debatable.' I note his name, and his sudden departure and what seemed to trigger it.

'Well now.'

Which is assigning it considerably more significance than I think is justified at this point. 'We shouldn't be jumping to conclusions.'

'I saw the T-shirt. I couldn't read it all.'

I give her the full picture, with a straight face. 'I think the guy is just wearing it for a laugh. Probably picked it up in some second-hand store for a couple of bucks. Probably has a stack of T-shirts with oddball parodies. Thinks it's cool.'

'Or he's born again.'

'And pushes someone to her death in a fit of religious fervour.'

I should know better than to dismiss Mae's suggestions. Either I'm a slow learner or I can't help myself.

'It's called brainstorming,' she says.

I bounce back. 'Absolutely.' Although the bounce is strained.

She works at appreciating the effort. She's making allowance for the pressures of the last two days. She's being generous.

Jake (alias Babe) is not mentioned again during the remainder of the ferry crossing. And we don't encounter him. Whether he's worked at escaping my attention could be open for discussion, but isn't. Neither is he mentioned on the drive from the ferry terminal to Forteau.

We check into Grenfell B & B. Peggy and Mae find lots to talk about. Caffeine-fuelled, I reboard the Durango and point it in the direction of the police station, unencumbered by notions of who did what to whom, and what the consequences might be. In other words—open mind, deep breath.

Soon to be over and done with and out the door. Romantic getaway intact.

DIM THE LIGHTS

WHO'S THE FIRST person I lay eyes on when I step inside the RCMP detachment in Forteau? None other than the freaking Heinz-shirted, note-taking ex-companion of the abruptly departed—Jake. Alias Babe.

What the hell?

The joker who elicits the question is blatantly less grungy. The hair has been tamed. Surrogate jeans, fully intact. And a replacement T-shirt, white and mostly hidden beneath the now-buttoned plaid shirt. No scruffy backpack. Except for the brawn, he could almost pass for nondescript.

Hate to tell him, but cops are predisposed to looking past the exterior to what is going on in the brain. In fact, it appears they are about to begin doing exactly that.

Corporals Larsen and Beauchamp are no longer the sole occupants of the detachment. I detected the door to Larsen's office being repositioned from the inside—I assume by another officer, and presumably the one from St. John's. I don't ask.

'Please take a seat, Mr. Synard,' says Larsen, sounding particularly regimented. 'We will meet with you shortly.' He turns to the other individual awaiting his attention. 'Mr. Moe, if you would, please step inside my office.'

Moe. Rather than Mow, or Mough, I assume. Moe as a surname is odd enough. (Mae, I predict, will find it particularly bizarre.)

In any case he takes precedence. I sit and wait. It appears they have much to talk about.

I could fill my time exchanging texts with Mae and Nick but choose not to. Fruitless speculation would only magnify the tension with upper-case replies, sharpened by multiple exclamation marks. That I could do without.

Instead, I turn my mind as far away from the present circumstances as I can manage.

That would be into the world of whisky. In my experience, always soothing to a troubled mind.

It's in anticipation of my return to the world beyond this interrogative detour. Back to the life that includes pairing an exceptional whisky with a well-chosen book. I can't wait.

In that other, regular life I partially fill my off-hours with the writing of a whisky blog, known to the wider world as "Distill My Reading Heart." (An inspired title, if I do say so.) I read, taste, and write about a whisky–book combination, an offbeat way to amuse myself, perhaps, but as I like to say, it makes my spirits soar.

During my preparation for this tour, a book caught my eye—*Stargazing: Memoirs of a Young Lighthouse Keeper* by Peter Hill, about the author's summer jobs on three remote islands off the west coast of Scotland. (Rocky, windy, and lots of sea spray, not unlike Newfoundland, I was thinking.) Tagged as both "sublime" and "salty" in the same review. The perfect choice— my assessment at the time.

After the subsequent lighthouse overdose, I'm not so sure. In any case, I ordered the book online and it should be waiting for me when I get back to St. John's. If nothing else, it will be a functional epilogue to the drama that has been the *Right On!*

Light On! lighthouse tour.

As for the whisky, I'm thinking both sublime and brine. And naturally I'm thinking Islay, home port of more sublime whiskies than any other place on earth, and where its single malts live for their salty peat profiles.

As I continue to wait for the call to the inquisition, my phone leads me to the Newfoundland Liquor Corporation website to see what might be hiding on the shelves, awaiting my return to the city. The NLC can't necessarily be counted on to measure up to expectations, but on occasion it surprises me with something extraordinary at a hefty but reasonable price tag.

Straight for the Whisky section, then the Limited Time subsection. Quickly past the bourbons, ryes, and Johnny Walkers of the world. To something peaty and decidedly eye-catching! Not Islay, but a close second. The box that holds the whisky glows with rugged red rocks and pounding blue surf.

Talisker Storm.

Powerful and Smoky. Brooding Spice. Made by the Sea.

More than enough to excite the whisky fiend. But then, inscribed on the box: "Feel the intensity rise as the storm sets in . . . The Isle of Skye powers through our veins and invigorates our souls . . . So raw, yet so refined."

I can only pray there's at least one left on the shelves when I get back to St. John's.

Staring at the closed door of Larsen's office, I still see no indication that I'll soon get the call. I glance over at a stone-faced Beauchamp. Nothing.

Thoughts of single malts cannot soothe a troubled mind indefinitely.

In this case, a troubled and conflicted mind. Okay, there's no denying that the situation with Marco (who must be in a holding cell somewhere in the bowels of the detachment) proved a bugger for me to get past. And now one Jake Moe has been dragged into the picture. That I've muscled aside as well.

Let the cops handle it all. That's what their federal pay-cheques are for. They sure as hell make more money than I do. I start another tour in two weeks. I need to get on with my other life, with making a living.

As for Marco, I assume he has hired Colin Baxter by now. If that doesn't work out, let him hire some big-shot criminal lawyer from wherever. He doesn't need me.

Get this interview over and done with and get the hell away from here—the one and only option as far as I'm concerned. As contrary as it might be to what Mae has in her mind. As much as it might trigger more aggravation between us.

Let's take the long view here. There are investigations that need me, and others that don't. There's no outright evidence of murder. Suicide is still very much a possibility. The woman had issues—that's obvious. That's where the focus needs to be— on her past, on what went on in her life that made associating with men like Marco and Jake seem like a good idea. Are the cops probing her family for answers? Are they widening the investigation to get to something beyond the catwalk of the bloody lighthouse?

The answers, by the sound of what's transpiring behind the closed door, is no. The exchange started as muffled and broken and now has hit intense. One phrase reaches me intact.

'You're fuckin' kidding me!'

I stiffen involuntarily. Déjà vu. An echo of Marco.

'I'm calling a fuckin' lawyer!'

Unbelievable. And very unreligious.

So much for the Catch Up T-shirt. I'm left baffled by the thought of just who Jake Moe has turned out to be behind closed doors. And by what line of questioning could have preceded the outburst.

The door flies open. Moe is manhandling his phone. I could suggest a lawyer, but refrain. He appears to know who to call. He smacks the phone against his ear.

'I need a lawyer.' Pause. 'Yes, Anton, a fuckin' lawyer.' He downs his phone and barks, 'I have the right to do this in private.'

He appears to know his rights rather well. Larsen directs him to an empty room. Larsen re-enters his office, then huddles with the person inside. No chance of their discussion reaching my ears.

Abrupt evening drama in the Forteau detachment. Which only heightens when an overly confident Moe reappears and is informed that he is being detained, pending further investigation. And yes, he has a right to remain silent until his lawyer arrives.

Who, it appears, will be flying in from St. John's sometime tomorrow. I recognize the name of the law firm. Their services don't come cheap. Sounds like whoever he called has plenty of cash to make it happen.

For now, much to his consternation, Jake Moe will be taking up residence in the detachment's area of confinement. Presumably there is only one such area, meaning he'll be sharing living space with Marco Tolentino. That could prove interesting.

'Mr. Synard, if you would.'

It snaps me back to my own set of circumstances. It's the call for me to take centre stage, the tone a touch overbearing, to my mind. There's no need, gentlemen. You're cops, I get the picture. I take a chair inside the office. We're all in this together, are we not?

Evidently not.

'Inspector Lockwood, Sebastian Synard.' Larsen's straight-up, no nonsense introduction.

The prompt for a stiff, hurried handshake. The inspector is all business. Larsen sits, Lockwood remains standing.

'Let's get right to it.'

No preliminaries, Inspector? No acknowledgement of the fact that I was the one to alert the RCMP to what happened? No thank you for all the information I have delivered to its officers thus far?

'It appears, Mr. Synard, that you have been previously acquainted with Jake Moe.'

It jars me, unnecessarily. Previously acquainted? 'You mean on the ferry? Not exactly acquainted. We met, very briefly.'

'He says acquainted. He says you knew him.'

'I thought it might be him, from the description by the man in West St. Modeste. Which I previous told Corporal Larsen about. As you know.' I look over at Larsen. He nods, slightly. 'During the ferry crossing was the first time I laid eyes on Jake Moe. Or him on me.'

'Not according to Jake Moe.'

'You're joking?'

I should know better. Interrogators don't joke. And that's what he's sounding like—a flippant bloody interrogator.

'He says he saw you at the Point Amour lighthouse.'

What the fuck?

'He's lying.' It's all I manage to get out. I'm still recovering from the shock.

'According to him you were standing outside the lighthouse when he arrived. That you appeared agitated.'

'I did not see Jake Moe at any lighthouse.'

'He didn't say that. He said he saw you. That you were "*very* agitated," to use his exact terminology. He said you were on your phone to someone you called Marco. That you told him you would quote "handle it," that everything was quote "under control." Jake Moe told us he withdrew from the scene and didn't engage with you for fear of physical confrontation.'

On the phone to Marco! Physical confrontation! 'I have no idea what the fuck he's talking about.' Excuse the fucking terminology.

'That, Mr. Synard, is something we are attempting to determine.'

'He's lying. He made it up.'

I dig out my cell and toss it on the desk in front of him. 'Here. Take a look at the numbers I called.'

Lockwood picks up the phone and examines it. He looks at Larsen. 'This is not the phone described to us. Would you agree?'

Larsen does. Lockwood turns back to me.

'Do you happen to own a second phone? Silver case. Somewhat larger in size.'

Well, fuck.

'And he described what you were wearing. Which has been corroborated by Corporal Larsen. How would Mr. Moe have known that?'

"Mr. Moe," is it now?

'I don't bloody well know. What are you implying, that—'

'We are not implying anything, Mr. Synard. We are conducting an investigation to ascertain the facts. The fact is Jake Moe says you emerged from the far side of the lighthouse as he was approaching from the parking lot. At which point he withdrew from the scene. Although not before he texted Amanda Thomsen to ask if she was all right. To which he received no reply. Such a text was found on the deceased's phone.'

Jesus.

'And, yes, the entrance to the lighthouse was locked, at the point that the Corporal Larsen and Corporal Beauchamp arrived.'

I'm stiff with frustration. Why pounce on me? Why the bloody hell should I be the one on the defensive?

'Yes, it was locked. And yes, it was locked when I arrived.'

He says nothing. Which means he's saying a goddamn lot.

'You will appreciate the fact, Mr. Synard, based on your knowledge of police procedure, that it is necessary to investigate every possible angle. We are developing a timeline here, to ascertain who knew what when, as well as their whereabouts at any given point in time.'

He finally takes a seat. 'Inspector Bowmore says to say hello by the way.'

What the hell? Jesus.

Inspector Bowmore, whom I've known from previous cases, is in on the act? When I think about it, I'm not surprised. Lockwood has been flown in from RCMP headquarters in St. John's. Where Inspector Bowmore is top dog. She has sent one of the assistant canines who hasn't been fully trained as yet.

'Please pass along my regards.'

'Mr. Synard, just to be clear.'

What now?

'You are not being accused of anything. We have no reason to disbelieve the sequence of events as you have related them to us. I might not need to do this, but I will do it anyway. I'll remind you that any information related to the case, no matter how trivial it might appear, needs to be communicated to us. I am fully aware that you are a private investigator.'

What else did Inspector Bowmore tell him? Not everything about our relationship, I'm sure.

'However, that gives you no privilege to withhold whatever you might discover, no matter how inadvertently.'

'That goes without saying.' I have no control over the snap in my response. The inspector, to judge by the intensity in his eyes, thinks I could have done better.

'Am I free to go? I assume you have no reason to detain me.'

'For now,' he says curtly. 'We could contact you at any time. If we have questions, we would expect an immediate response. According to Corporal Larsen, you'll be close by for the next few days. In cellphone range, I assume.'

'As far as I know.' Equally blunt and to the point. I let it hang in the air.

It's pressing my luck, but Lockwood needs to get it in his bloody head that I'm due more respect, that I'm central to this bloody case. His workmate, Ailsa Bowmore, should have plenty good to say about me. (Our extracurricular activity, while brief, was mutually exhilarating as I remember it, and ended without acrimony.)

'It would be in everyone's interest if you told me why Mr. Moe is being detained.'

Inspector Lockwood peers at me. He sees absolutely no reason to agree. He does, however, hesitate.

'Corporal Larsen, perhaps you would like to respond, given you have spent more time with Mr. Synard than I have.'

Somewhat more promising. Larsen, nevertheless, is in a bind. He might feel I deserve to know, but he's also feeling the need to play the tough guy, for the benefit of the inspector.

'Let's just say his story doesn't make complete sense. Not at this point at least.'

'How do you mean?' I don't give up easily.

Extended hesitation. He eventually glances at Lockwood. Do I detect an appreciable widening of the inspector's eyes, which for individuals in his position might the equivalent of a slight nod? Am I to assume that Inspector Bowmore did indeed put in more than just a modest good word for me? That, in fact, she had been rather positive in her comments about my character and, yes, of my abilities as a PI?

'Mr. Moe, although he says he saw you, did not report his

concerns to the detachment, even when it became public knowledge that Amanda Thomsen was deceased. We went looking for him, I would add, on the basis of the information you provided. In the meantime, he had crossed back over to Newfoundland.'

Larsen glances again at the inspector. This time there's no eye movement.

Nevertheless, Larsen has something else to add. 'Mr. Moe, in the course of our questioning him, has suggested that, based on your state of mind at the lighthouse, you and the person he says you were speaking to on the phone may have colluded to do harm to Amanda Thomsen.'

That son-of-a-bitch.

'When Corporal Beauchamp and I arrived, which would have been at least ten minutes later, you were in fact somewhat agitated.'

'I had just discovered the mangled body, goddamnit!'

He says nothing. He's not about to take it any farther.

It's far enough.

Just what the hell did Moe have to do with Amanda's death? That's the fucking question, rationally stated.

Without going so far as to rephrase it to: Did the lying son-of-a-bitch murder her and is he trying to bloody well pin it on me and Marco? Which is what is storming its way around in my head.

Needless to say, this changes everything.

In a few minutes, I'm back at the Grenfell B & B. Not enough time to calm down, let alone decide what to do from here.

Instead of going inside, I head to the fireless firepit and park myself in one of the Adirondack chairs. I stare into the pit, my back to the house. I ruminate.

So much for exorcising the lighthouse tour and getting on with life. So much for the damned romantic getaway. Fuck.

I need control. I need to lay out options and nail down a rational decision.

Put aside the fact I'm being accused of murder. Even if it is by some hare-brained asshole.

See what I mean? Shift emotion to the back burner and it comes back to burn your ass, every time. Fuck.

'Is something wrong?'

I didn't notice her coming.

'I heard the vehicle drive up.'

'You better sit down.'

She's surprisingly calm, reluctant to ask more questions. She's putting them on hold, waiting for me to frame whatever story is about to emerge. I'm grateful.

I keep it straightforward, matter-of-fact, stripped, as much as possible, of bloody anger and frustration.

When I stop, she takes a noticeable pause before saying anything.

'Well, shit.'

She's in control. "Well, shit" is level-headed. I could learn a few things.

'What are you going to do now?'

'Huge question.'

'Or should I say what are we going to do now? I'm with you whatever you decide.'

'Thanks.' Not much of a response, I realize. I lean over and kiss her.

She rises out of the chair, then sits in my lap. She wraps her arms around me. 'I love you,' she says, tightening her embrace.

I reciprocate, without words. Searching for some, not finding what I'm looking for.

'Peggy said there's leftover soup in the fridge. We're welcome to whatever else we can find. Let's have supper, then sleep on it. It'll be clearer in the morning. You'll be in a better frame of mind.'

Not so sure about that. She's still in my lap. A good position to convince me.

We wander to the house. Soup, salad, homemade bread, a hot shower, and Laphroaig.

Even at that, sleep doesn't come quickly.

Not that I'm much interested in making out, at the beginning at least, given all that's still hurling through my head. Mae believes otherwise. She works at it, slowly, but then rather meticulously.

I come around to loving the meticulously. To the point of vocalization, encouraged by the fact that we are the only occupants of the B & B. A type of muffled primal scream therapy.

It does me good. Climax sets loose the mind, enough at least that my head settles.

We sink back into the bedclothes, shuffle about to lie seamlessly against each other, and sleep on it.

YELLOW LIGHT

THE ROMANTIC GETAWAY survives, redrafted but intact.

It's now a romantic getaway/criminal investigation. I've managed to get in touch with Marco through his lawyer, Colin Baxter. I asked him to let Marco know that I'm reconsidering his offer.

The message back from Marco was, to quote Baxter, "Whatever it fucking takes." Which I take to mean I'm hired. I'll give him a cut rate, given I'm out to save my own skin in the process.

Baxter has no problem with sharing the load. 'Whatever it takes,' he says. A lawyer with a sense of humour. That's good. He's going to need it.

Mae, Gaffer, and I have crossed the Strait of Belle Isle, back to the island. We'll stick to the upper part of its Great Northern Peninsula as we'd planned, in case the RCMP in Forteau get in a sweat and order me to take up residence in their detachment.

On a calmer note, we've settled into the accommodation Mae had booked for us, a mere day past the original arrival time. The owner was notified and, considering we weren't looking for any adjustment of the rental fee, welcomed us with open arms as well as a half-dozen fresh-from-the-oven rolls and a jar of blackberry jam.

I take it as a good omen. We've escaped (for the moment at least) to the simpler things in life—rugged coastlines, spruce-scented trails, pan-fried cod, fresh rolls and jam. All the while quietly engaging with the colourful past of the French Shore . . . with the thought that this would very likely be a place Amanda Thomsen would have come to, given the scope of the book project she was working on.

Conche is an outport of a hundred and fifty inhabitants on the eastern tip of the peninsula. For four hundred years, French fishermen crossed the Atlantic to fish for cod along nearby coasts, salted and dried it onshore, before sailing back to the markets of Europe. We can learn all about it from the story-boards and artifacts in the French Shore Interpretation Centre, but we're here most of all to feast our eyes on the community's famous tapestry.

Mae has seen it before, when it was on exhibition in St. John's, but not where it was conceived and embroidered, where this extraordinary sixty-six-metre tableau, inspired by the Bayeux Tapestry in Normandy, was hand-stitched on linen in a resplendent depiction of the history of the French Shore.

'Absolutely remarkable.' That's the less enlightened half of the couple speaking. My breath is taken away, my tour guide genes on overload.

'Take a panel, any panel,' says Mae, 'and focus on it alone. Let the details consume you.'

I'm working at it, until I find myself standing next to Joan Simmonds, the manager of the Centre, the resident of Conche most responsible for seeing the creation through to its comple-tion. 'Remarkable.' And that would be my assessment of Joan as well.

Remarkable but very upset.

'Vandalism. I still can't believe it. You must have heard what happened?'

We didn't—despite the fact, as Joan tells us, that it's been all over the news. Too many other things going on in our lives.

She fails to calm herself. 'A break-in. Can you believe it— some damn fool smashed a window and got inside. Thank God it was covered by plexiglass. I can hardly speak about it, I'm so hurt.'

'Vandalized? You mean sprayed the plexiglass with something?'

'No, marked it up. With a wide-tip, black, permanent Sharpie.'

There's a need to realign my brain cells. The damn fool desecrated the tapestry?

'And the police still haven't got a clue who did it. I combed the Centre myself, inside and out, after the Mountie had finished his search and left. Nothing.'

'Not a thing? Not one thing that struck you as odd?'

She draws her head back slightly. She's thinking. 'A clamshell box sticking out of the garbage. With what looked to me like leftover poutine. I didn't bother calling the Mountie. He would have only laughed at me.'

Dare I ask why a half-clamshell of poutine would be odd?

No need.

'Nobody I know would go to the trouble of going to Lumberjacks in Roddickton, buy an order of poutine, drive here, then throw half of it away. Unless, of course, he made a mess of it with the mustard. Dijon, by the look of it.'

Enough said.

'An indelible, wide-tip Sharpie,' says Mae, still not past her horror at the thought of anyone wielding such a thing at a priceless piece of fabric art.

'I know,' says Joan. 'Unbelievable. We were lucky it cleaned up with rubbing alcohol without any damage except for a few scratches on the plexiglass.'

That last fact is hardly any consolation to Joan. The mere thought that someone would even conceive of damaging the beloved tapestry will forever outrage her.

Nevertheless, the vandalism does give way to another matter that's also been all over the news. Once it becomes known that we've just crossed the Strait from Forteau, her attention abruptly shifts to the fatal fall at the lighthouse. She has good friends in southern Labrador and knows all about what happened. Or, more precisely, has been party to the rampant speculation that must have heated up the cell towers.

She's now expecting to be party to something more—the story from someone who was actually in the area when it happened. I hold back, not about to disclose the specifics of my connection.

'She was here, you know.'

'Amanda Thomsen, the deceased?'

'She came to take pictures of Conche and of course found her way to the Centre to see the tapestry.'

'How long did she stay?'

'The best part of an hour. We had a long chat. She was especially interested in the physical evidence of the French being here. I told her about the naval cemetery in Croque and the ship names carved in the rock.'

Amanda Thomsen was here long enough for Joan to be shocked and troubled by her death. She can't believe the young woman would have died by suicide or, God forbid, that someone would have pushed her over the railing. On the other hand, an hour was hardly time enough to understand the workings of Amanda's mind. Or a criminal mind behind her death, for that matter.

'Was anyone with her?'

'As a matter of fact . . .' Yes, a tall, note-taking young fellow with a head of curly blond hair. No surprise.

'Did he strike you as peculiar?'

'Peculiar?' She's not sure what to make of the question, or why I would be asking it.

I hesitate but in the end I put it out there. 'I'm a private investigator, Joan. I'm looking into the unexplained death of Amanda Thomsen.' Her expression changes from inquisitive to unnerved.

'Oh dear, I'm not so sure. No more peculiar than some I've seen.' She ponders it and I wait her out.

'Most people take their time and walk slowly along the full length of the tapestry, as Amanda did. Not him. He was in and out in ten minutes. When she finally left the Centre, she was texting him, I assume to meet up. When they left Conche they were going on to Englee, according to what she told me.'

'And when was the break-in, in relation to the day they were here?'

There's a pause while she thinks it through. 'It had to be that night.' Her expression reverts to inquisitive. 'You don't suppose—?'

'That they had anything to do with the vandalism? Not really.'

We don't need more rumours. My response is enough to curtail her chain of thought. But not my own. Let's just suppose Jake Moe did return to the Interpretation Centre, with or without Amanda Thomsen, and inflicted the Sharpie on the plexiglass. Why? For what reason would he engage in such a bizarre act of vandalism?

'Why?' echoes Mae, a short while later, when we're alone. A fundamental question, perhaps central to learning who the lying son-of-a-bitch really is.

And I thought we were managing to take a quick break from whatever the devil went on at Point Amour.

Gaffer has done his business and now we're all back aboard the Durango and heading for Roddickton, a town about a half-hour west of Conche, which, as Mae notes, happens to be roughly halfway between Conche and Englee.

According to Joan, the closest restaurant to Conche with poutine on its takeout menu is in Roddickton. We decide we might as well make it our supper stop.

Its full name: Lumberjacks Diner. It lives up to our expectations.

'I'll go with the Trucker's Special. Heaping order of fries, hamburger meat, onions, mozza cheese, dressing, and gravy. And for dessert the Chocolate Eruption.'

'Count me in,' says Mae. We both chuckle.

Our pretensions give way to pan-fried cod and salad.

'We'll skip dessert, Gina,' I say, glancing at the name tag of the young woman who takes our order, 'but we'll have a serving of poutine to go.'

An odd addition for us, but necessary to the investigation. And a tax write-off, even if it doesn't get eaten.

We stay only long enough to consume our meal. We're handed the clamshell box of poutine at the checkout counter as another, older woman rings in the bill.

'Anything to go with that? Most people wouldn't be caught dead putting anything on their poutine. But I always ask.'

'Mustard.' Most definitely.

Her eyes widen. 'Regular yellow or Dijon? Dijon is extra.'

She adds twenty-five cents to the bill and tucks a small packet inside the box.

'By the way, you wouldn't happen to remember, several days ago, someone picking up a takeout order of poutine—tall guy, bit scruffy maybe, blond hair.'

'Tied back in a bun?'

'Possibly. Dijon with his poutine.'

She pauses.

I think we just struck gold. I'm surprised, with so many customers coming through.

'Hot, as Gina called him.'

Hot and with Dijon. That explains it.

Back in Conche, I open the clamshell and lay it on the kitchen counter, then carefully transfer its contents to a plate to boost its visual appeal. To be honest, a heap of fries topped with cheese curds and brown gravy can only look so good on a plate. Its appeal, after two minutes in the microwave, is its aroma and taste. Sinful, yet irresistible.

Despite the fact that it may well be sacrilege to drizzle mustard on poutine, I'm out to replicate what Jake Moe held in his hand prior to flinging it in the garbage bin outside the Interpretation Centre in Conche. I do hold the Dijon to what I think I can stomach. Mae looks at me.

'I honestly don't have a problem envisioning him eating half and throwing what was left over in the garbage. What I do have a problem with is understanding what might have been going through his mind that would lead him to that absurd act of vandalism.' Her preoccupation hasn't changed any.

I, on the other hand, take up a fork and give it a go.

'Surprising,' I pronounce after the sampling.

Gaffer agrees. The mutt always did have a soft spot for poutine (minus the Dijon).

'Not as good as what I've had in Montreal, of course, but not bad. I'd take a pass on the mustard though.'

'Back to the basic question,' says Mae, demonstrating an urgency to get past the condiment. 'What was his motivation?'

'Exactly. What you're saying is that Jake Moe is an outlier.'

'In which case . . . ?'

'In which case we need to find out more about him. Ramp things up. Dig into his background.'

In other words: execute a social media hunt for the next hour, once the poutine is over and done with.

A social media hunt that comes up dry.

'Very strange, if he's trying to make a living as contract writer.'

'Obviously has no intention of playing by the rules,' Mae adds. 'Either he's shut himself off entirely from the wider world, or he writes under a different name.'

Even rerouting to Amanda's social media footprint leads nowhere. Her Facebook account, although it hasn't yet been deleted, is private. I take another look at her website, but it's limited to promoting her photography business. Nothing personal.

We close our laptops. 'Tomorrow is another day.'

'More ramping up,' says Mae.

'More digging.'

'In the meantime, Sebastian, the question is—can you really cut the mustard?'

A challenge if I ever heard one.

BEGINNING TO SEE THE LIGHT

OUR ROUTING IS the 430 to St. Anthony, where we'll take up new accommodations, and which is also headquarters for the project that both Jake and Amanda had been working on. I've managed to track down the project manager, someone by the name of Ruth Harris. The phone call to her is brief, marked by a mixture of grief and desperation. She's looking for answers. She thinks I might have some.

We've backtracked from Conche to the 432, which will connect us to the 430. But not before a side trip down the 438 to Croque. I like the numerical synchronicity.

'Some say Croque came from "croc," which means boat-hook, if you dig deep enough into ancient French.'

'Reinforces that French connection,' says Mae. 'Good for tourism.'

'I think Croque could up its connection significantly.'

'Really?' Mae senses an attempt at humour. She's prepared to not believe a word I'm about to say.

'Whenever I've eaten out for lunch in France, I glance over the menu and go straight for the Croque Monsieur. Gruyère cheese, shaved ham, Béchamel sauce, layered between slices of bread—I prefer sourdough—and grilled to perfection.'

'Very popular in France, I agree. As is the Croque Madame.'
Equal rights never far from her mind.

'Not just *very* popular. I would say *wildly* popular. As it
could be for tourists along the French Shore of Newfoundland.
I can see the tag lines now: "Come to Croque for your Croque
Monsieur! Only in Croque, your Croque Madame!"'

'Sitting on a gold mine and they don't know it,' Mae says,
shaking her head, and smiling broadly. It's the Sebastian she's
seen before and is relieved to see again.

'I'm serious.' And I am in a way. 'Look at how Dildo in
Trinity Bay capitalized on its name. Add a craft brewery to the
mix. Local beer with your Croques.'

'Hordes of tourists, all wearing Crocs.'

This woman is made for me.

It takes a while to return to why exactly we are venturing to
Croque.

Which is, as Joan in Conche pointed out, because Croque
was considered the capital of the French Shore and holds the
clearest physical evidence of the French connection. We're
working with the expectation that Amanda Thomsen and
Jake Moe showed up here not long after being in Conche.
What, if anything, they experienced in terms of human
contact might put a few more pieces of the puzzle in place.

Modern-day Croque has a population of forty-five, so not
a lot of possibilities. I'm betting on finding someone in the
vicinity of the French naval cemetery, where we have now
arrived. There are about a dozen graves here, from the time navy
patrols protected the French fisheries from the British and from
American privateers. I spot one marker dating from 1792.

The cemetery faces the harbour. Just next to it is a stretch
of several fishing sheds, painted ochre trimmed with white. It's
an iconic outport scene, made all the more so by a fisherman at
his splitting table, one hand encased in a filleting glove, his knife

intent on his morning's catch. We wander over.

'How's it goin'? A few fish on the go. Dandy weather.' It identifies me as a Newfoundlander, a good first step.

'Yes, b'y. As the ol' feller said, calm as a clock.'

A bit ironic, since he himself has more than a few years under his belt. Ageless in the way that he fits into the outport he's known all his life. He appears to welcome the break in his routine, all the while keeping up with the job in front of him.

He hauls another codfish from a tub nearby and slides it onto the splitting table. 'Where you from?' The sure-fire question.

'St. John's.'

'I won't hold that against ya.' He chuckles as he slits open the belly, removes the egg sacs (the britches, as they say), then tears out the rest of the entrails. 'Out for a look at the cemetery.' It's not a question. Clearly, it's the standard reason people show up in Croque.

'Very interesting,' says Mae.

'Yes, my love, it is so.'

He works at the cod's head, cutting away the tongue and the small pocket of flesh under the eye—the cheeks—that, together with the britches, make for particularly tasty bits when cooked right. He tosses them all into a small bucket.

'Up until the '70s, a French Navy ship would show up most every year to tend to the graves. Since they stopped coming, we tries to keep it up ourselves.'

'Lots of people stopping by?'

His attention turns to filleting the fish.

'I wouldn't say a lot. We're a bit out of the way, you know. The ones who read about it beforehand, they're usually the ones what show up.' He takes time to sharpen his knife, expertly flicking a whet steel rod back and forth against the blade.

'Wouldn't have happened to notice a young couple, several

days ago now? She'd be taking lots of pictures. He was tall, head of blond hair . . .'

He finishes the sharpening. 'Working on some kinda project?'

'That would be them.' We've struck it lucky again. 'She was the one who died in that fall at the L'Anse Amour lighthouse.'

'Yes, b'y?'

His way of wondering aloud why I'm asking about the pair. With slick manoeuvres of his knife, he cuts away the flesh from the sound bone that runs the full length of the fish.

'We're working with the RCMP to find out all we can about their whereabouts prior to the accident.'

He stops the filleting and looks directly at us for the first time.

'No uniforms?'

I'm tempted to say we're working undercover, but who knows where that might lead.

'Private investigators.'

His inquisitive eyes twitch slightly.

'You mean, like *Mannix*?'

That dates him. Even older than I thought. 'Not exactly.'

'*Shakespeare and Hathaway* then?' He grins.

I've heard of it. I think.

Mae leans my way. 'BBC.'

'I watch it on BritBox,' he tells her.

He's back to the task at hand. He flips the fish over and sets to work filleting the opposite side.

'Did you notice anything about them? Anything unusual?'

He's considering an answer. The cod has been relieved of all its edible parts. He tosses the carcass over the wharf and into the water, alerting the trio of seagulls that have been circling nearby in anticipation. He lines up the two fillets in front of him, flesh side up.

'Unusual? You could say that. I 'spose if you was into what they calls "meditation," maybe not.'

Mae and I share looks of bewilderment.

'That was my reaction. Even though I seen him sitting on a yellow mat in the cemetery, like what my granddaughter in St. Anthony got for her yoga class. Him wit' he's legs curled up under he's arse and moaning like he had something caught in he's throat.'

The man's a born storyteller. He takes a calculated pause, allowing us time to fathom what he's said. Building the suspense.

'So then the girl come over. I was standing right where I'm standing now. She said who she was, asked if I minded if she took a few pictures. "Go ahead, my love," I told her, "Take all the pictures you wants." Then I nodded my head toward the graveyard. "What's he at?" I said to her. You know, curious, like you would be. "Meditation," she said. "Calming hesself down."'

He returns to the fillets while we continue to fathom. He works the blade of the knife under the flesh at the tail end of one, just above the skin, then, taking hold of the tip, glides the blade flat against the skin all the way to the other end. Slick as a whistle. He dispatches the skin into the water, then cuts away the line of small bones that lies against the thickest section of the fillet. And there it is—a priceless, boneless fillet of Atlantic cod. I would be imagining it sizzling in a frying pan, if my mind was not otherwise occupied.

'"What's he calming hesself down from?" I says to her.'

As if the momentum of the story had never been interrupted.

'"He has this thing about graveyards." That's what she said and went off then snapping her pictures.' He stops, focusing completely on the story for the first time. 'You two thinkin' what I'm thinkin'?'

I expect we are. This thing about graveyards? Who has "this thing about graveyards" then plants himself in one?

'Takes all kinds,' he concludes. 'He got up after a spell, rolled up he's mat, and walked back to their car. I got a good look at him. Strappin' big fellow and at that stuff? Makes no sense. I coulda used one he's size last winter, up in the woods, cuttin' logs.'

Could have used his brawn for sure. As for his brain, that's debatable. Just what has been going on in Jake Moe's head continues to mystify me and there's nothing that our fisherman informant can do that will help the situation. He's reached the end of his story.

We forgo the slimy handshake, but I thank him and wish him well. 'We're Sebastian and Mae, by the way.' After the fact, but it would be rather ungrateful to depart as strangers. It would only add to his cynicism about townies.

'Eddie,' he says.

'You've been very helpful. We really appreciate it, Eddie.'

'Short for Édouard.'

Mae's ear for local pronunciation is better than mine. But even she hesitates. 'You mean, like Édouard Manet, the painter?'

'No, like Édouard, the Frenchman buried in the cemetery.'

Yes, why let us go without another eye-opener of a story?

'When the French Navy showed up in the harbour, they'd often have a doctor aboard. They'd tend to the graves, but they'd also tend to the people here what had medical problems. Father had an abscess on he's tooth, and the feller pulled it out wit' he's pliers. Put Father out of he's misery and he was so thankful that when I was born the next year, he figured he'd name me after a Frenchman in the graveyard. He and Mother had trouble pronouncing it, like you would. So I was always called Eddie.'

'Amazing, Eddie.'

'Yes, Édouard,' adds Mae, 'Amazing.' I would say Eddie hasn't been called Édouard in a very long time. He smiles broadly.

And on that note, we say a last goodbye. We wander back to the Durango, with a brief detour for a closer look at the names in the cemetery. Sure enough, there's Eddie's namesake: *Édouard Villaret de Joyeuse, Officier de la Marine Française*, who, according to the marker, died in 1854. The name's a mouthful that I leave Mae to articulate.

We do a thorough scan of the graveyard, just in case Jake was up to something other than meditation.

He sure as hell was, if we're safe in attributing what Mae believes are marks left by a "wide-tip, black, permanent Sharpie" on the picket fence that encloses the graveyard. The top of each picket is not flat, but pointed, a decorative feature resembling an arrow. On a half-dozen of them, a black marker has been used to outline its pointed edges, then used again to add a vertical line down its centre.

Six black arrows pointing skyward.

My conclusion? The tag for Jake doing meditation: lead me to heaven.

Mae's conclusion? The tag for Jake doing drugs: take me higher.

We have a second site to check out before leaving Croque. The walking trail to get us there is in desperate need of repair. Its boardwalk and stairs have rotted and fallen away in several places, leaving us no choice but to circumvent them, negotiating our way down inclines over loose and jagged rocks.

We are, nevertheless, determined to make it there, and eventually do.

It's worth the danger pay. In rock faces at the end of the trail, French sailors and fishermen have carved the names of their ships and the year they showed up in Croque. The inscriptions have become weathered and blackened with lichen over time, but, with effort, are still quite readable.

'1862 ROLAND.'

'POMONE 1868.'

Each inscription is several inches high, so carving them was no small task, especially with nineteenth-century tools.

'I'm surprised some modern-day idiot hasn't tried to add his bit.'

'You spoke too soon.' Mae points to a lower corner of the rock face, somewhat removed from the predominant inscriptions. It's smaller, a bit rough given the pitted surface, black like the lichen, but sure as hell discernible.

'Well, shit. The asshole, at it again with the marker.'

This time he's drawn what looks like a tree with three upward branches.

'Forget the damn meditation, forget the damn drugs. We're bloody well missing something here.'

It takes her a moment. 'I agree.'

Asshole defaced an historic site. And, unlike with the tapestry stunt, nobody shows up with rubbing alcohol.

'Say it was Jake Moe who did it.'

I let that go. Of course it was Jake Moe.

She continues, 'If he was really out to deface the site, he could have attacked the engravings themselves. No plexiglass this time.'

'Nevertheless . . . he broke the bloody law. Why?'

'Why? Exactly.' She adds, 'To me, it has elements of a hate crime.'

What? 'Against people who lived more than a century ago?'

'There's got to be more to it than that.'

'Agreed.' And I say it again, 'Agreed . . . But what the hell, what?'

Tell me we're not going around in circles.

We reach St. Anthony with a couple of hours to spare before our meeting with Ruth Harris. The circling continues. We've just set off on a 1.5 km hiking trail that loops around to its starting point.

'Splendid views, I promise.' I could use splendid. As well as 'restful and steeped in history.' Mae has made a calculated choice to up the interest level of her human companion.

The non-human companion is not a cynic. Gaffer is, in fact, eager. For him, this excursion is a reprieve from another stressful morning inside the Durango. For me, it's meant to be a reprieve from another stressful morning outside the Durango.

It's called the Tea House Hill Walking Trail. Aware that additional incentive might be needed, Mae quickly notes how well it ties in with our stay at the Grenfell B & B in Forteau. The trail starts and ends just behind the house (now a museum) designed and built for the famous Wilfred Grenfell and his wife.

'Anne MacClanahan,' Mae informs me. 'She was an heiress from Chicago, twenty years younger than her husband. They met aboard the *Mauretania* in the spring of 1909, on the way back from England. Within six months they were married.'

Good to know. We leave it at that.

The trail, as I abruptly discover for myself, leads to the couple's final resting place. Ten minutes into the hike, I'm standing face to face with the rock wall into which their ashes have been interred. Mae had decided the surprise might put a firm end to my lethargy.

It is a bit of a shocker, actually. I hadn't expected to be suddenly staring at the bronze burial plaque that commemorates a man who, in the opinion of this history major, comes closer to sainthood than any figure in the history of Newfoundland and Labrador. It takes a moment to rebound and bring myself back to the here and now.

'No graffiti, thankfully.' Although I suspect Jake Moe has been here. And Amanda as well. It had to be on the list of sites included in the project.

'He had his limits.'

'No connection to France or French fishermen,' Mae points out. Her hate crime theory endures.

I refrain from arguing, largely because I have no theory of my own to counter it. We walk on. The lookouts offer impressive panoramic views of St. Anthony. I would almost go as far as "splendid."

I reserve that for the Grenfell House Museum. Rarely have I walked into a home and been immediately excited at how it set me back in time, how it stirs my imagination. The wraparound sunroom, racks of caribou antlers looking down as the doctor sips his morning tea. The living room with its polar bear rug set on dark, polished oak, young children stretched across it in the flickering fireplace light. The bustling kitchen filled with the aroma of bread baking in the oven of its wood-burning stove. And best of all, the narrow, book-filled office where I find Grenfell clacking on his typewriter, writing books that have found their way onto my own bookshelves.

Mae draws her share of excitement from the bedroom upstairs, from Mrs. Grenfell's dressing gown, which hangs next to an open wardrobe. Sheer pink silk trimmed with wide, delicate lace. Sumptuously Edwardian.

'Beautiful fabrics, beautifully detailed,' she says.

'Amazing.' I'm not being facetious. Such fashionable luxury is not something you associate with outport Newfoundland of a century ago.

'She was Grenfell's counterpart, very much alike in some

ways, very different in others. They were a good match, it appears.'

Mae smiles and looks at me in a way that I've seen before and which I can never interpret with confidence. She has more on her mind than fabrics. Or the intricate pattern of the hand-stitched white quilt that covers the bed.

We've not talked directly about how good a match we ourselves have forged. I prefer what I think of as building a relationship by osmosis. We spend time together, we experience various situations, and over several months the relationship takes hold (or not). It unfolds naturally, without the pressure of commitment. Enjoying the moment, confident the rest will fall in place. Let it find its own rhythm, move along at its own pace.

We have each gone through a relationship that at one point we considered permanent, but which, in the end, wasn't. Divorce puts a damper on commitment, I find.

Grenfell House Museum is not the place to take on such personal points of discussion, despite our being in a bedroom, and the only visitors at that. Time to move on before it gets crowded.

'I like the lace effect on the pillows,' I say, moving toward the door. 'Made for some interesting pillow talk I would imagine.'

I glance back at Mae. She smiles again. A bit more controlled this time.

PARADISE BY
THE DASHBOARD LIGHT

THE FACT IS we have a very important rendezvous. There's only time enough left to take Gaffer for a quick walk before sitting down to a cup of seafood chowder—the "world-renowned, mouth-watering specialty starring local Coldwater Shrimp," as the menu modestly notes—on offer at the Lightkeepers Café.

It is served with a side order of the Fox Point Lighthouse, framed by the picture window adjacent to our table. As if I hadn't had enough of lighthouses already.

Although a tidy, attractive red-and-white wooden tower, it is confirmed by Google to be vertically challenged at a mere eight metres. Nothing that would have sustained the interest of the pharos four.

'They turned you into a lighthouse snob,' Mae says. I'm pleased to see a more familiar smile.

But credit where credit's due: Mae came up with an eating establishment that puts me in the conceptual state for what is about to unfold. A half-hour later, we are parked in front of the nondescript bungalow that I gather serves as both accommodation and project headquarters. I suggest we both turn off our phones to avoid interruptions. We bargain with Gaffer for a longer walk at some point in the future, then head inside for our encounter with what is sure to be a distraught project manager.

'The Point Amour lighthouse is over a hundred feet high.' She has trouble getting the words out. 'I have nightmares of her falling that far.'

Mae gives Ruth a hug, a mere two minutes after they've met. I'm never less than mystified at how quickly demonstrative women can act on their empathy.

I notice that Ruth Harris has yet to make the transition to metric, a telling detail in my mind. Canada converted in 1975. Her mind is grounded in the 1960s, as confirmed by the braided grey hair, the plaid shirt and denim, and the fact she's lived most of her life on a "heritage farm" near Kitchener, Ontario. It would seem to me she went back to nature and never really left.

Except to come to Newfoundland and Labrador and, over several visits, fall in love with the place. Her husband passed away, her son took over the farm, and as a lover of books and the arts, she transitioned into what is known in the publishing industry as a "book packager." She comes up with ideas for books, sells the proposed package to a publisher, then undertakes all the work involved and delivers a manuscript ready to go to print. The initial few were coffee-table books about rural Ontario, and it seemed natural that she would next come to focus on the second area of the country that was very familiar to her (and, let's be honest, significantly more captivating than the first).

She tells us all this in segments, interspersed with a pattern of deep breathing in which she stiffens her back and broadens her shoulders while pressing the thumb and forefinger of each hand tightly together. I can't say I was ever big on yoga myself.

The conversation sets the background, a necessary exchange but one that also serves to calm her down. To a point, that is. After all, one of the two people she hired is dead, and the other is in police custody with the implication that he may have been responsible for the death of the first.

'How did you come to hire them, Ruth? Did you know them already?'

'Amanda I knew from the images she produced for Parks Canada. She had several contracts with them to photograph various sites for their publications. Some very fine work.'

Entirely reasonable.

'As for Jake, he came recommended by Amanda. He had a limited publication record, but the magazine articles I did read were impressive. They were both from Newfoundland, of course, which I felt was important. Given I wasn't from here myself, I knew it would help sell the project.'

She's right there. We've had more than our share of mainlanders showing up and misinterpreting our province. But let's not go there.

'Were they a couple when they started work with you?' asks Mae.

'Not that I was aware of. And I'm not sure "couple" is the right word. They kept separate bedrooms from the time we all moved in here. Of course, they were back and forth most nights. Which is only natural. You know.' Adding, matter-of-factly, 'Who wouldn't? Jake is pretty meaty.'

Meaty? What era is that from? At least she didn't call him a beefcake.

'I know what you mean,' says Mae.

She does? And with a straight face no less. I think she's trying to get a rise out of me. Stay on topic, folks.

'From your perspective, Ruth, did their relationship change over time?'

'I sensed something was up with them before they took the ferry to Labrador. There was no outright argument, for me to see at least, but she was giving him the cold shoulder, definitely. Of course, they still had to work together. I was the one who booked accommodation for them if they were away from St. Anthony. Normally they let it be known that they were fine sharing. But in this case, they asked for separate rooms. And they each took their own car, unlike other times when they would take just one.'

A love affair gone bad? As I suspected.

'We know Amanda stayed at the Grenfell B & B in Forteau. What about Jake?'

'There was only one room available at the B & B. I booked Jake into the Florian, also in Forteau, as you probably know.'

More than probably know. And more than a bit surprised.

The asshole, large as life, was down the corridor somewhere while Nick and I and the pharos four, including Marco, were all reading menus in the Florian's restaurant.

Or was he? More likely he was prowling about Point Amour trying to convince Amanda to let him inside the lighthouse. More likely he was gearing up to have it out with her, having witnessed Marco exit the lighthouse late that afternoon.

There's no reason to let Ruth in on any of this. Better to move on before the raised eyebrows are noticed.

'And he came back to St. Anthony that night, the night Amanda's body was discovered?'

'Surprised me. Crossed on the last ferry, said he didn't need to stay in Labrador, that he had all the information he needed. He sat at the table and ate the takeout he had picked up on the way here, and then went off to his room, I assumed to work on an account of the sites they visited in Labrador. Then the next morning I got the call from an RCMP officer in Forteau about Amanda's death. He called back an hour later, once I told Jake and had time to recover myself. He asked quite a number of questions. When we finished, he asked to speak to Jake.'

That would have been after Larsen and I had our talk. Jake crossed back again on the ferry the next afternoon, which is when Mae and I encountered him.

'You wouldn't by chance remember what was in the takeout he brought?'

Not a question she's expecting. Nevertheless, she has a ready answer. 'Poutine. He loved the stuff. Loved it with Dijon mustard. Couldn't understand it myself.'

Nor is she expecting the self-congratulatory look Mae and I give each other.

'So, Ruth, what do you make of Jake, overall?'

She takes another deep breath, without the yoga components this time. 'We all have our idiosyncrasies, I suppose.'

Yes, you could say that.

'I wouldn't call him peculiar, per se.' Another noticeable breath.

Keep going.

'I will say this.' Pause. Breath.

I assume we'll get there eventually.

'Jake kept files. Of his encounters. With women.'

'That's interesting.' What I really want to say is, "How do you know this?"

'Really?' says Mae. 'How do you know this?'

Better coming from a woman in any case.

'About an hour after Jake left to catch the ferry I went to his room. I'll admit it was an invasion of his privacy. Definitely not something I normally would have done. But given what had happened . . .'

I could say that, given what had happened, she might have been tampering with evidence.

'It was before the RCMP got back in touch to say I should close the doors to both bedrooms and leave them closed until someone from the detachment in St. Anthony arrived to search them. Which they did later that day.'

'They also discovered the files no doubt.'

'And took them away. I have to be honest, I didn't tell the RCMP I had read them. Well, some of them, enough to get the gist.'

A prolonged gist, I wouldn't be surprised.

'What do you mean by "files"?' asks Mae. 'Do you mean notes?'

'In a journal. One of those Moleskine notebooks, hard-cover, pocket size.'

'I know the kind,' says Mae. 'Sebastian uses one.'

For something other than erotica, I might add. But don't. I refrain from turning the focus on me.

'Most of the pages were ruled, but some of them at the back were blank. Well, not really blank. He had them filled with drawings. Quite graphic. He was very good at depicting the human body, actually. If you ignored the details.'

Which she obviously hadn't.

'So most of it was a journal, I take it?' Mae continues. As I said, better coming from a woman.

'He sometimes wrote other things. But from what I could tell, he wrote an entry not long after each encounter.' She hesitates. 'Again, quite graphic, actually.'

No doubt. The gist goes on.

'Twice in the Mini Cooper. Which must have been a bit of a challenge, given his height.'

I think we can stop at that.

'You might be interested in the last journal entry. The one I think he must have written the night he came back.'

'I was wondering if there might be one,' Mae says to her.

I would have been, too, if Ruth hadn't been so focused on the graphic.

'It wasn't long. Only two words. Neither of which I'm sure if I'm even pronouncing correctly.'

'Give it a try.'

'Fokka Tolentino!' She then spells each word. 'Exclamation point at the end.'

Exclamation point is right. So the bugger definitely knew about Marco.

Amanda did tell him. When? Earlier in the day? Or when he got to the lighthouse? And in his jealous rage Amanda ended up over the railing?

As for "fokka," I'm thinking it's Jake's stereotypical Filipino pronunciation. "Fokka Tolentino!" with suitable hand gesture, kind of like faking Italian.

'Possibly Old Norse,' says Mae, fresh off Google. 'Possibly the origin of the word "fuck."'

Really? Who would have thought it?

'He's nonconformist, I'll say that much,' inserts Ruth, apparently excited at seeing investigative work in action.

'In what way?' asks Mae.

'Well . . . for example . . . we spoke English most of the time, but, when they were together in a bedroom later at night he would sometime verbalize in another language—which, frankly, I didn't understand. Loud and uninhibited actually, especially as he neared what I could only assume was the . . . well . . . I was surprised at how many different words he used, actually.'

It appears that Ruth had been kept entertained. Whether that semi-salacious tidbit is of any importance is, to my mind, an open question. Vocalization in such situations is not uncommon.

Ruth's phone rings. A welcome relief to us all. We can do with a pause in the action.

'Hello,' followed by a prolonged period of intense listening to the voice at the other end.

'Good God!' Ruth exclaims.

More listening, more intense.

'No, there's been no contact.' The deep breath I have been anticipating. 'Yes, I have met him. As a matter of fact, he's here right now . . . Yes, I'll tell him to phone you. Right away.'

Phone who? What's this all about? The call ends.

'You're not going to believe this!' Inhale, exhale. 'Jake has escaped from custody!'

'He what?'

'He and another guy somehow managed to tackle the corporal who was on duty in the detachment. They took off in Jake's car, left the officer bound and gagged. He was only discovered when Corporal Larsen came into work this morning. Later than usual. He'd gone to Red Bay on other police business. By the time he got back to Forteau, they'd been on the run for more than six hours.'

Ruth was bowled over but is recovering. I'm still floored.

'You need to call Corporal Larsen. On his cell,' she tells me. She checks her phone and relays the number. 'There's a possibility they crossed on the eight o'clock ferry without anyone realizing who they were.'

'You mean they could be on the island somewhere making a getaway?' asks Mae. A dramatic but decidedly rhetorical question.

'To where?' That's my question, and it's not one for which there's a ready answer.

'I don't think they would show up here,' says Ruth.

'Agreed.' There would be no point. 'They might want to take you hostage, but that would be too risky. Too many people would recognize the car.'

While Ruth deals silently with the image of herself bound and gagged in the cramped back seat of Jake's vehicle, Mae and I brainstorm other possible scenarios.

We agree with Larsen, who seems to have ruled out the possibility that the renegades tried anything other than taking the ferry to Newfoundland. The road into Quebec past Blanc Sablon hits a dead end after seventy kilometres. Blanc Sablon has an airport, but even if there was an early morning flight, everyone in the area would know about them by the time they got there, and they wouldn't have made it past the check-in counter. Likewise, no point in driving the Trans-Labrador Highway. At least eight hours to get to the airport in Goose Bay, let alone the seven more to reach the Quebec border. Too long on the road. Too many potential police blockades.

'The ferry was their only choice. Sounds like they got lucky and made it across. I'd say then they headed down the peninsula. Maybe to try flying out of Deer Lake.'

That's Mae's opinion. I have serious doubts. 'Say the eight o'clock ferry left on time. Add however long it took to disembark, and you're talking ten o'clock at least. Then a minimum three hours to Deer Lake, and who knows how long to the next flight off the island. It's a small airport with only a few flights a day. No way can they avoid being intercepted by local cops.'

'Or go on to Port aux Basques and catch the Gulf ferry to Nova Scotia.'

Even less likely. 'That's another three hours from Deer Lake. In which case. . .'

I take out my phone and check the time. 'They would be arriving right about now. The cops in Port aux Basques will be checking every vehicle in the lineup for the next crossing. The timing's definitely off.'

That ends the proposals on her part. I have one. 'Their ultimate goal has to be to somehow get off Newfoundland. Get to the mainland, and from wherever they land to keep on going—fly, drive, whatever—BC, the States, Mexico, who knows. There's only one place in Newfoundland where they have any chance of making it off the island unnoticed. And that would be St. John's.'

'Déjà vu.'

A subtle allusion to a previous case in which the evildoers raced to St. John's and hid out there, scheme in place to escape to the mainland. And they might have pulled it off if I hadn't thrown a very large monkey wrench into their plans.

At this point, the scenario I've handed Mae is still all so much speculation. We can't be sure where the hell Jake and Marco are or where the hell they might end up.

'Until the cops come up with a lead as to just where they might be, there's bugger-all we can do.'

'Like a sighting? Like at a gas station? They absolutely have to stop for gas,' says Ruth, who, listening to Mae and me bounce opinions back and forth, is keen to get in on the act.

'Exactly,' says Mae. She looks pleased to see a female perspective counter what she perceives as pessimism.

It is not pessimism. It's common sense. Which I know better than to say out loud.

'As you see, there are multiple possible scenarios. It doesn't make . . . it doesn't work in our favour to pursue one that might then take us so far away from where the action is that we lose crucial time backtracking.'

'So your approach,' she says, rather stiffly, 'is to wait, to do nothing?'

'Not nothing. When I contact Corporal Larsen, I'll have a better feel for the situation. He may see an immediate role for me.' Awkward pause. 'For us.'

'Defer to the police. That's not like you.'

No longer subtle. Definite sarcasm. Accompanied, however, by a smile. Of sorts. Which is good.

Let's take a breather. I glance at Ruth. 'Any coffee on the go, by chance?'

It readjusts her focus. 'Sure. I'll put on a pot.' She heads into the kitchen.

'Regular or decaf?'

'Definitely regular for me,' Mae calls to her.

By this time of the day, I usually switch to decaf. I find I get a better night's sleep.

'Sure. Regular sounds good to me.' For the sake of unity.

It's definitely a good point at which to call Larsen. I take out my phone.

'Let's see what the Forteau corporals are up to.' Nonchalantly, keeping it positive. I look at Mae and point my head toward the kitchen.

'I'll just step outside.' Mae gets the picture.

The fresh air is very welcome. I consume a copious amount before making the call.

'RCMP. Corporal Larsen.' Not the disciplined yet comradely tone the Mounties usually like to project.

He must have seen the caller ID. Undoubtedly, there's a great deal occupying his mind.

'You asked me to call. Sorry to hear about what happened.'

'We had what could be a sighting.' The empathy was a miscalculation. He's all business.

'Good to hear.'

'At a gas station, outside Flower's Cove. Not where you'd expect, and not positive. A Mazda, the attendant thinks, parked, waiting for the station to open. Could have been grey. He's not sure. Only one guy aboard, he thought, but that means nothing. The second guy could have been hiding somewhere, waiting to be collected after the car was gassed up. The guy in the car might fit the description of Marco. The attendant wasn't sure. It was his early morning shift. He might have been half-asleep or hungover.'

Tenuous. Sketchy. I'm surprised Larsen is so forthcoming. It's clear he's desperate for all the help he can get.

'That means they headed north when they got off the ferry,' I am deliberately confident. 'Further up the peninsula.' Rather than south, which everyone here was betting on. And Larsen, by the sound of it.

'Not sure it makes sense. But it's what we have to go on at the moment. The three detachments north of the ferry termi- nal are all onto it of course. The airport in St. Anthony is under surveillance.'

That might sound good, but I suspect it doesn't amount to a whole lot of Mounties. And spread over a couple of hundred kilometres at least. Larsen's desperation is increasingly apparent.

'How can I be of help?' With a slight note of deference. Always a good strategy.

'I wouldn't be doing this except that you're informed about what we're dealing with.'

To say the bloody least. Okay, okay, keep your cool. Let it unfold on his terms.

'You know both the fugitives. Give it some thought. If, in fact, they've confined themselves to the top of the Northern Peninsula, then where would they likely have gone? Head there, check it out, ask around in case anyone meeting their descriptions were in the area.'

Exactly what I would have done in any case.

'Good idea.' Forced out.

'I got to go,' Larsen says.

'How's Corporal Beauchamp doing, by the way?'

'He's back at it.' Call ended. Larsen is done and gone.

Beauchamp went through a tough several hours. Tough and embarrassing. Still, the corporal sounds resilient. The Mounties always get their man. Dollars to donuts, the slogan has wormed its way into the youthful Beauchamp's head and lodged there permanently.

Before going back inside, I release Gaffer from his confinement to do his business. The dog is overjoyed, to put it mildly,
only adding to the guilt that continues to build over the
fact that he's being left in the vehicle so much of the time. He
is a patient mutt, but he has his limits. He's desperate for
the outdoors, so I take him for a quick walk. He does not
appreciate the return to the Durango. Treats have lost their
charm.

'That was a long call,' notes Mae as I re-enter the house.
She and Ruth are sitting in the living room, sipping fresh coffee.

'Gaffer needed exercise.'

'You have a dog with you?' says Ruth. 'And you left him in
the vehicle?'

'He's used to it,' I lie.

'Bring him in. I love dogs. The poor pooch, stuck there all
this time.'

I do as I'm told. Immediately on my return, Gaffer, tail
waving at warp speed, runs joyfully about the house, then
makes for Ruth, planting his front paws in her lap, ignoring
the caregivers in the room. Gaffer has always known on which
side his bread is buttered.

I have treats in my pocket. I hand some to Ruth to portion
out to him. The treats have suddenly recouped their charm.
Then I get to the much-anticipated report on the phone call.

'You were right, Ruth. It all came down to a sighting.'

'Yes, I knew it. I can picture exactly what happened.'
Having read more than a few crime novels in her time, I suspect.

'This is all confidential, by the way.'

'Of course. We wouldn't want to undermine the CSI.'

Yes, and more than a few TV crime shows. None set in
Canada, given her use of the acronym. The reference, however,
does invoke a bit of local trivia from me.

'Did you know that Sid Hammerback, the medical examiner on *CSI: New York*, was played by a Newfoundlander? Bob Joy.'

'Not true! I loved that character. Loved his glasses.'

'There's so much trivia about this place that we even have our own board game. It's called *Newfoundlandia*. Like *Trivial Pursuit*, only on a lesser scale.'

Ruth is impressed. Mae, not so much. She holds back, but I'm getting the message. To my credit, I did avoid mentioning we also have our own five-volume *Encyclopedia of Newfoundland*. Close to four thousand pages.

'Okay.' Mae is now staring at me, impatiently. Time to move on. 'Where do we go from here? That's the question.' She turns to Ruth.

'Is there another place with a distinct tie-in to the French Shore that we don't know about? And that Jake hasn't gone to? There's something about these sites that seems to attract him.'

Mae's been thinking. I quickly step up to the plate. I inform Ruth of the places on the French Shore we've already visited, avoiding, however, sharing the suspicions we have about what Jake has likely been up to at each site.

'So you haven't been to Album Rock?'

I glance at Mae. I'm safe in saying, 'We've never heard of it.'

'It was on the schedule. Jake and Amanda would have gone there later this week.'

We need a broader perspective here. What is this Album Rock that fell below our radar?

Ruth seems to relish the notion of informing a bred-in-the-bone Newfoundlander about an historic site on the island that he's never heard of. Fortunately, in recent years I have become somewhat magnanimous. I'm more than capable of ignoring the ego and focusing on the facts.

These are the facts according to Ruth. 'A huge rock on the shoreline of Ship Cove, north of here. It was the subject of one of the earliest known photographs taken in Atlantic Canada.'

Might I point out—this is not a particularly earth-shattering nugget on which to base an historic site.

'The photograph was taken by French naval officer Paul-Émile Miot in the late 1850s. Remember, the first known photograph taken anywhere dates from 1827, which just happens to be the year Miot was born.'

The man had a full thirty years to get his act together.

'The photograph is rather bizarre, actually. It takes a while to figure out what exactly is going on.'

A bit of nineteenth-century weirdness. I can't wait.

'It shows a small group of French sailors painting huge capital letters on the face of the rock to spell the word "ALBUM."'

I cough at this point, to underscore the conclusion that whatever sense this makes qualifies it at best for entry in some obscure, amateurish compilation titled Weird and Wacky Facts about the French Navy. You sure as hell don't find it in the five-volume *Encyclopedia of Newfoundland*.

'Album?' asks Mae, to repeat the obvious.

'As in photograph album,' says Ruth. 'The speculation is that Miot, once he got back to France, would have used it for the cover of the *album* of photographs taken on the voyage.'

'How interesting,' says Mae. Over the top, to my mind.

'Absolutely,' says Ruth. 'I like to think of it as one of the greatest rock albums of all time.'

I smile. Magnanimous still, but under significant strain. A near buoyant Ruth says nothing but exits the room, returning quickly with a copy of the infamous photograph. She passes it to Mae, the more supportive audience member.

'Wow,' says Mae. 'That's quite something.' She scans the photograph for details. 'There's a fellow in a white shirt, holding a paintbrush, finishing up the serif on the last letter.'

Serif—a new one on me. A significant detail, I'm sure.

'Now I see—he's standing on a ladder above a ledge. Incredible!'

She passes the photograph to me. 'Have a look, Sebastian. You'll be amazed.'

Not to put words in my mouth, I'm sure. I hold the eight-by-ten and flip to the back side. *Rocher peint par les marins français*, followed by the photographer's name. And officially stamped *Library and Archives Canada / Bibliothèque et Archives Canada*. I flip back. Printed from a glass plate negative, I presume, including the plate's damaged corners. The central image is intact, but dark and indistinct. I give it my full attention, as expected by the onlookers.

Yes, the white letters are prominent, serifs and all. Meticulously painted, I admit, considering the roughness of the rock face. Notable as well is the figure of a man standing on top of the rock, silhouetted against the sky. I turn my focus to the M. 'Yes, the guy is on the ladder, bucket of paint next to him.'

'Look closer,' says Ruth. 'You'll see there are two more sailors, one kneeling on the ledge under the space between the U and the M, the other at the base of the rock posing with what looks like a staff, or perhaps a mop.' I do as directed.

Mae eagerly joins me on the couch so she can see details that passed her by. I hand her the photograph, having now noted all four (awkward-looking) Frenchmen.

Mae lowers the photograph and turns to Ruth. 'We're at a loss for words.'

I bite my tongue. Simply put, any harder bite and I would take a piece out of it.

'How long a drive to Album Rock?'

'The final stretch of road can be a bit rough. You're talking forty minutes at least.'

Mae turns to me. 'Let's go and take a look. If Jake's been there, he might have left some clue.'

Clue? To what? Haven't we had enough of this Sharpie crap? What's she thinking—there's a smoking gun on some rock? Leading us to what went on at the lighthouse?

She's waiting. Looks like I'll be keeping my two cents' worth to myself. I settle for a shrug.

'Sure.'

She turns to Gaffer: 'Time to make a move, Bubba.'

The dog is equally unimpressed. He slinks closer to Ruth with a questioning look in his eyes. What's with these people? Why back to Durango prison? I only just got here. Did I re-offend?

As it turns out, Ruth thinks of herself as a bit of a dog whisperer. And is a generous one at that.

'Leave Gaffer with me. You two go and do your thing and I'll take care of him. Won't I, Gaffer?'

The clever dog answers with an affirmative yelp and a celebratory tail wag. Suddenly an alternative to the guilt of returning Gaffer, the disgruntled dog, to vehicular confinement.

'That's very kind of you.' Not that I want to be seen as jumping at the chance, 'You're sure?'

She is. And with that Mae and I are soon heading outside.

'We won't be long, I'm sure.'

'Take all the time you want.' At her side Gaffer yelps and waves his tail goodbye.

FLASHING LIGHTS

ALBUM ROCK IS to be found along the shoreline of the afore-
mentioned Ship Cove, which, as Mae takes care to point
out, is the most northerly community on the island of
Newfoundland.

'That in itself is reason enough to visit it,' she adds. She
knows I have a predilection for geographic landmarks. Add to
that the fact it is (let me be the first to admit) picturesque,
and there you have it—more than enough reason to set aside
my skepticism for the moment and make the most of the
walk that will, in its own good time, bring us to face to rock
face with the momentous mass.

'Look,' declares Mae, 'I think that must be it.'

She could be right, given there is no other stand-alone
rock along the shoreline that measures up. Nevertheless,
there's no need to get prematurely excited. As it is, I'm anticipating disappointment on her behalf.

We're approaching the rock from the side opposite the
one the photograph depicts, should it in fact be the rock in
question.

Mae makes one-word affirmations the closer we get. 'Yes.'
Then 'Righto.' A brief pause. 'Absolutely!'

We turn the corner around its innermost edge.

'Fuuuck.'

That would be her monosyllabic cohort's contribution. It's Album Rock, all right. With several letters inscribed on it in bright white paint.

Not the original ones of course. They weathered away a century ago. Besides, these letters are half the size.

'Sans-serif,' says Mae.

Is there any need? No. Because it's the word, not the letters, that's causing me to expand the expletive.

'What the fuck?'

ALBUMET, it declares.

I think we're past the point of debating who put it there.

'What's with the asshole Jake? That makes no sense!'

'Maybe it was meant to be *album et*, but he wasn't careful with the spacing. And he got scared off before he was finished.'

Dubious in my opinion.

'Maybe ET is code for something?'

'Extraterrestrial?' She shrugs.

'I was thinking ET—Enemy Territory. I saw it in a book once. I think.'

'Or it's from another language.' She hurriedly retrieves her phone. Then hits a cellular wall. We're out of range. Not a single bar of coverage.

There's no point in lingering at the impenetrable rock. We take a few pictures, including one with me standing next to the ALBUMET, for scale. Up close and personally frustrating.

We are back on the road to St. Anthony, Mae behind the wheel, me fiddling with my phone every couple of minutes. Finally "No Service" gives way to one, then two bars of signal strength. Will Google Translate do anything but muscle me into a foreign language maze? I urge it not to.

'C'mon, c'mon, detect language.' Finally, Google coughs it up.

'Norwegian.'

'Norwegian?'

'Holy shit . . .'

'What?'

'Translated to English, ALBUMET means . . . you're not going to believe this . . . it means ALBUM.'

'It's Norwegian for album,' she confirms, if only to sharpen our attention on the sudden twist in the narrative.

'Why Norwegian? Maybe Jake's Norwegian? Moe always struck me as a kinda odd, outsider name.'

Back to Google. It takes a while.

'Yes. Number forty-seven on the top one hundred list of surnames in Norway.'

'Jake doesn't sound particularly Norwegian,' Mae points out.

'Short for Jacob. In Canada, he shortens it to Jake.'

'Jacob doesn't sound particularly Norwegian either.'

My brain cells defy all expectations.

'Jacob with a k. Jakob Ingebrigtsen. Phenomenal runner. From Norway. I watched him win Olympic gold.' I take a breath and smile. 'We're good, Mae, we're very good.'

'So Jakob Moe has Norwegian roots. What's that got to do with defacing historic sites on the Northern Peninsula of Newfoundland?'

Precisely. This is where the brain cells must not only defy all expectations, but pillage and plunder in the process.

'When I say Norse and Northern Peninsula, what immediately comes to mind?'

'L'Anse aux Meadows, of course. Vikings. Anne Stine Ingstad.'

'Exactly. Except I would have said her husband, Helge.'

After all, Helge Ingstad was the modern-day Norwegian explorer whose persistence led to the discovery of Vinland, to

what became the only authenticated Viking site in the New
World.

'Because of him, we know that Leif Erikson and his Norse
comrades sailed into L'Anse aux Meadows five hundred years
before Columbus hit the beach in the Bahamas.'

'I always felt his wife got the short end of the stick. She
deserves equal credit. After all, Anne Stine Ingstad was the
archaeologist whose work led to the discovery of the bronze
cloak pin and the spindle whorl that proved conclusively
the Norse were here. Including women, spinning fleece and
weaving cloth.'

That explains it. Mae has always been big on textiles.
However, I know better than to argue.

'In any case, the point is—Jakob Moe is Norwegian,
the Vikings and their discoverers were all Norsemen . . . and
Norsewomen.'

'His connection sounds tenuous,' she says. 'It could very
well be a coincidence.'

Let me ruminate on that for the moment. Is Mae, in fact,
the voice of reason? The more logical of the investigating duo?
The rumination continues.

My iPhone in hand, it's back to Google. Search terms: Moe,
Ingstad, Norse, L'Anse aux Meadows.

A few weak-cell-signal moments. Followed by, 'Sweet
Mother of God.'

Mae's hands tighten around the steering wheel. She antici-
pates a jolt.

'Anne Stine Ingstad's name before she married in 1941—
Anne Stine—'

'You're kidding?'

'—Anne Stine . . . Moe.'

'No way.'

'And . . .' I read on. 'And . . . Jesus, Mary, and Joseph . . .

she married Helge *Marcus* Ingstad.'

Mae slows the Durango, eases onto the shoulder of the road and parks. She turns to me.

'Jake short for Jakob. Marco short for Marcus. This is not a coincidence.' The rumination comes to an end.

'I'll call Ruth. We'll be delayed.' There's a slice of urgency in my voice.

I make the call. Mae turns back onto the 437, which intersects with the 436, at the end of which is Vinland, now known as the L'Anse aux Meadows National Historic Site/UNESCO World Heritage Site and one helluva big deal for anyone with two clues about world history.

'When the Norse landed in L'Anse aux Meadows, they encountered the Indigenous descendants of the peoples who first came out of Africa then migrated east across Asia, across the Bering Strait and into and across North America. The Norse, meanwhile, were the descendants of the peoples who had left Africa and migrated *west*, across Europe, across the ocean to Iceland and Greenland. For the very first time, the circle of human migration was complete. The moment they met was an amazing landmark in human history.'

Even if Mae knows this already, she embraces it.

'In the same way that Jakob, migrating from Norway, meets Marco, migrating from the Philippines,' she continues. 'The circle is once again complete?'

'Exactly.'

'To be truthful, Sebastian, it sounds rather hokey to me. I think you're off the rails with this one.'

That stung.

'Just trying to be honest,' she says.

Yes, just. I suck it up and decide to say nothing. We're getting closer to L'Anse aux Meadows. I've bet the farm on what we'll find when we get there.

Then again, maybe we'll find sweet fuck all.

Okay, it more than stung.

'I'm sorry,' she says. 'Love sometimes hurts.'

Really. There's no need. My silence continues. Which could be interpreted as petulance. So be it.

And the slow burn continues to the parking lot of the site at L'Anse aux Meadows. Besides a large tour bus, there are several vehicles in the lot. I quietly scan them. She knows what I'm looking for.

And knows when I find it. Maybe not sweet fuck all after all.

I make no reference to the grey Mazda. In fact, I ignore it as we start the walk along the path that leads to the Interpretation Centre. I know there's one helluva lot of grey Mazdas in the world.

'Bit chilly for this time of the year,' she says. 'I imagine it can get quite cold here in winter.'

When in doubt, talk about the weather. Always a reasonable option in Newfoundland.

'Very exposed. The wind chill always a factor.'

Of course, the weather is not what's on our minds. Along the path is a high granite plinth bearing bronze busts of the Ingstads gazing over the landscape where the Norse settlement was confirmed. *Anne Stine og Helge Ingstad* is carved into the stone, in a stylized, Scandinavian-looking font. And below the names: *De oppdaget vikingenes Amerika*, which would seem to confirm their discovery.

'Very nice,' Mae comments. A peace offering, of a sort, given she makes no mention of the fact that Anne Stine's name precedes that of her husband.

We move on to the double glass front doors of the Centre, only to find several people, obviously tourists, standing outside.

'Parks Canada isn't letting anyone in. We've been told there's been an "incident," whatever that means.'

I press ahead to the door and peer inside. Calm enough. I see a sole Parks Canada employee walking about, that's all. The "incident" appears to have triggered a mass exodus.

I knock firmly on the glass. The fellow keeps his distance. Responds only with a hand gesture telling me to stay away. Something weird is definitely in the works. Have the fugitives hurled Parks Canada into a panic?

There's got to be a way to get to the other side of the building. I nod to Mae to follow me and we withdraw, quietly so no one is likely to follow, back up the path to the Ingstads.

Taking direction from their gaze, we head onto the scrub-covered rocky landscape. The goal is to round the near side of the Interpretation Centre to where a boardwalk begins. I recall it from a visit several years ago. It will pass under a monumental bronze sculpture erected to commemorate that landmark moment in human history. Sculpted in two parts by Luben Boykov and Richard Brixel, it's called *Meeting of Two Worlds*.

The boardwalk then winds its way through the archaeological dig site, ending in a cluster of reconstructed sod houses. That's what I anticipate.

Anticipation is slammed by absurdity. It stops us dead in our tracks.

The *Two Worlds* have met anarchy. We scramble toward it. We hit the boardwalk and within seconds reach a stunned cluster of tourists and Parks Canada staff. Both components of the sculpture have been scaled and, perched partway up each, is a wacko dressed in Viking garb, ranting at the audience below.

My first, unfocused thought is that the pair are part of some re-enactment crew staging bizarre theatrics. Part of some avant-garde arts festival, cultural funding gone off the rails.

Not so. Through war-painted faces peer the eyes of rene-gades. The why and wherefore of our landing in this epicentre of Viking history.

Jake and Marco. Jakob and Marcus. Take your pick.

Either way, they'd have you believe they're a fearsome duo. Jake's blond hair, released from its man bun, is in full disarray, notwithstanding the polished steel, riveted helmet he wears. He's shed his T-shirt in favour of a bare, tattooed torso, shoulders cloaked in the skin of some hapless forest beast. Jeans replaced by coarse woollen trousers, feet encased in calfskin wrapped and tied halfway up his shins. Both wrists thickly clasped in engraved silver bands.

Ditto for Marco, who must have shopped at the same online Viking shop. Ditto except that from his helmet protrude a pair of horns. He couldn't resist the added drama, despite the fact that everyone knows the Vikings didn't really wear horned helmets.

And ditto except for the handheld weapons. Jake wields an axe, Marco a sword. Nicely crafted. Must have cost them a pretty penny.

All pretentious swagger. They put me in mind of someone. I can't remember who.

Despite the balls needed to set themselves on display like this, it comes down to two questions. Why show up here, when the cops will be storming onto the landscape at any minute? And, more to the point, just what the bloody hell are they up to anyway?

Come bloody hell or high water, they're up to no good.

'Hail Vinland!' shouts Jake.

'Hail Vinland!' echoes Marco.

They raise their weapons in the air. 'We meet in the name of revolution! East meets west. We define civilization!'

'We reshape it to what it was meant to be. In the name of Odin!'

In the name of odious is more like it. What is this—they're obsessed with a world ruled by rogues and pillagers? They're so out of touch with reality they haven't got a jeezly clue they're making fools of themselves?

'These two are murder suspects for fuck's sake,' I mutter under my breath to Mae.

'And white supremacists.'

It hits me. She's right. Now I remember. That guy with the animal skins and horns storming the US Capital. A chest clogged with tattoos.

Jesus. I think his name was Jake.

'They appropriate Viking symbols,' says Mae. 'I saw a news segment about it on CNN.'

Two Jakes with the same pecs tattoo—three interlocking triangles.

Jakob Moe, a.k.a. Jake Moe, imagined Ingstad relation, embraces Viking symbolism to reinforce his white supremacist mindset. Somehow teams up with Marcus Tolentino, a.k.a. Marco Tolentino, and the pair plan the staging of a demonstration at the ultimate Viking site in North America. Not even murder put them off.

'Until Valhalla!' shouts Marco.

'Until Valhalla!' echoes Jake.

Not soon enough.

I hear the tramp of boots behind us. Everyone looks back. Sure enough, the cops are coming. A camouflaged squad of four in full riot gear—helmets, shields, batons, sidearms. One sniper rifle.

An overreaction. But kudos for intimidation tactics.

Everyone pivots back to catch the renegades' reactions. Only to be left dumbstruck by the sight of a costumed clan of four, racing toward the sculpture from the opposite direction. They must have sprung free from the sod houses at the end of the boardwalk. Four Parks Canada Vikings—two women, their long skirts hoisted up to free their legs, and two men shouldering a long pole, chopped to a sharp point at one end. Maybe a stake from a stockpile used for fence repair, who the hell knows? Wherever it came from, it's the weapon of choice. One better than a baton, two parts shy of a battering ram.

The pounding of the Mountie tactical boots drowns out what little noise Viking foot-leather can make. Jake and Marco don't have a clue that they're about to be ambushed from behind. A brilliant marauder move.

The Norse men come to a halt and lower the pole into their hands—surprisingly, with the broader blunt end forward. The Norse women take hold. The four swing the pole back and forth three times before taking aim.

Jake's butt is the first point of contact. His axe goes flying, as does he—flat on his face on the boardwalk at the base of the sculpture. Marco only has time to turn around before he gets it in the gut. His sword goes flying, as does he—flat on his back on the boardwalk, within arm's length of his co-conspirator. By the time the riot squad reach them, they're two flattened Vikings, still very much alive but not about to re-enact anytime soon.

The police squad lower their shields. Their batons hang limply at their sides. They look vaguely disappointed.

The Parks Canada Vikings, on the other hand, are more than pleased with themselves. It was an admirable performance, well beyond their job descriptions. One would think they're due a boost in pay.

In the meantime, RCMP backup has arrived in the form of four more officers. Two, I assume, from the detachment in St. Anthony—who quickly check on the escapees, and two recognizable as the super-stressed Corporal Larsen and the still somewhat chagrined Corporal Beauchamp. It would appear they temporarily vacated the fort at Forteau and crossed the Straits to be closer to the "sighting", and action central.

Corporal Beauchamp eagerly attaches the handcuffs. While Larsen and the other officers debate whether there is a need for ambulances, I get a good look at Jake's silver wristbands. One in particular stands out. It's elaborately engraved, with what looks like a stylized 'n' accented in gold. Set him back more than a few kroner, I would say.

Jake and Marco struggle to their feet, a surprise to everyone, which quickly resolves the ambulance question. Only then do I step forward and make my presence known. Larsen is moderately surprised to see me.

'What the hell, Synard. You figured out they'd be here?'

'Myself and Mae.' I introduce her.

'We uncovered some clues,' she says to him.

'Which I didn't have time to relay to you,' I quickly point out. 'We need to talk.'

Which definitely won't be right away. Limp, bruised, and battered, the fugitives manage to dredge up whatever resilience they have left and direct it at Corporal Larsen.

'I told you—I didn't do it,' rails Marco. 'She fell, that's all. I didn't fuckin' push her.'

She fell, that's all? How bloody pathetic is that. How bloody hard-hearted.

Larsen is having none of it. Marco's expletive didn't help.

'Get them in the wagon,' he tells the riot squad that's standing by, in limbo, anxious to be doing something useful.

'Me neither,' barks Jake as they seize him. 'What the fuck? She wasn't being careful.'

Wasn't being careful? The woman was killed because she wasn't being careful? How bloody hare-brained.

'You got to believe us,' yells Marco, now in my general direction.

I heard that one before. And look what that led to.

'It was an accident,' he yells. 'It was her own fault.'

The squad, two to a prisoner, drag them off past the wide-eyed cluster of onlookers. Literally drag them off—apparently they haven't the strength to walk on their own. The quicker the idiots are shut up in the wagon, the better.

The officers from St. Anthony inform everyone remaining that they are to assemble in the Interpretation Centre. There are questions to be asked, statements to be taken. The officers have a private, and noticeably serious, word with the local combatant Vikings. As impressive as they were, vigilantes are frowned upon by the police. Had the escapees been seriously injured, there would be hell to pay. I'm thinking the Vikings just might need a lawyer. I could save them the trouble of looking and point them to one Colin Baxter, although it's likely the guy's small-town-lawyer skills have already been stretched far beyond their limit.

Mae and I are about to join the crowd heading to the Centre when we're approached by a young woman holding, of all things, a microphone.

'Would you mind giving your reaction to what happened here today?'

'You're a reporter?'

'For the *Northern Pen*.'

The *Northern Pen* is the weekly local newspaper. No doubt this would be the biggest story to hit their front page all year.

'Do you mind telling me how you came to be here?' I ask. It couldn't have been happenstance.

'A call came into the office.'

They were tipped off. By one of the two renegades, undoubtedly. What's a protest and a plea of innocence without a wider audience? It's not the *Globe and Mail* or CNN, but it would have to do.

'I managed to get a few video clips on my phone,' she says, with a distinct measure of pride. 'Who knows where they'll end up.'

She's right. When I think about it—wider coverage than I would ever have thought possible.

'No comment,' I tell her, now getting straight to the point. The last thing I want is to be in the public eye over this.

She's not easily put off, but I smile and pull away. She redirects the mic to Mae, who is equally reticent, thankfully. The reporter shrugs and moves on, desperate to hit at least one tourist with no resistance to sixty seconds of questionable fame.

It seems to us that, for the time being at least, the lustre has gone off the UNESCO World Heritage Site. I'm sure it will return, once the police have gone and it reopens to a public unaware of what has taken place.

The boardwalk meets a set of stairs leading to an observation deck just outside the doors to the Centre. I insist we take a moment to renew and refocus. I put an arm around Mae's waist and draw her to the railing and the panoramic view of the monumental site. We didn't get to experience its significance the way the Ingstads might have liked, but for a few moments we can imagine doing so.

'Just think,' says Mae. 'This is where Gudrid gave birth to Snorri, the first European child born in the New World.'

'And just think—the Norse kid encountering an Indigenous kid and the two becoming best buds.'

'You might put it that way,' she says. 'That was the meeting of two worlds. Something to hold onto. Not what we just witnessed.'

For us, the RCMP questions can wait. The police have enough on their hands at the moment. We agree to meet at the station in St. Anthony first thing in the morning. We can all use time to make sense of the idiocy of the last hour.

Mae and I try to do just that during the drive back to St. Anthony to pick up Gaffer.

'The tattoo with the three interlocking triangles—it's called a Valknut.' I hold my phone closer. 'Get this—"Valknut wearers believe that they will be empowered to overcome any ups and downs in life with the aid of Odin."'

'Don't we all. Have our ups and downs,' says Mae. 'Some people look to God. Others to a god in Norse mythology.'

'Really? You'd give Jake that much credit?'

'No, I can't forgive his beliefs. Absolutely not. What I wonder about is what led to them.'

'What about what they led *to*? Murder. Amanda Thomsen is dead because of his beliefs.'

'We can't say that.'

'I just did. You're not saying she's dead because she wasn't being *careful*? C'mon.'

'I'm saying that until there's a trial and a jury decides otherwise, there's always going to be questions. Maybe it was an accident.'

'Right. You're buying into his story, a story he's concocted to save his ass.'

'Okay, okay, let's pull back for a moment.'

Good idea.

Before long Mae turns off the road and into a parking lot.

'I'm hungry. Are you?'

Clever move. We both know what pressing my buttons can lead to. Besides which, we haven't eaten since breakfast. She's turned into Dark Tickle. They're famous for their jams and jellies made from wild Newfoundland berries, but Mae also knows them for their bistro.

The cod chowder is excellent, as is half the ham and rhubarb-pickle sandwich that Mae can't finish. She's saving room for the partridgeberry and bakeapple ice cream in its fish-shaped "sculpin cone." I have one of those, too. Actually, when Mae's had her fill, I polish off the rest of hers as well. It pays to skip lunch sometimes.

What's equally impressive is the atmosphere. It's a bit of a museum, with artifacts from the days of the French migratory fishery along this part of the Great Northern Peninsula—what fishermen from Brittany and Normandy called *le Petit Nord*. Another part of what to us has become the infamous and storied French Shore.

'I'm surprised Jake didn't stop off at Dark Tickle and do his thing,' I say when we're back on the road.

'It was probably on his list. Ran out of time.'

We're being facetious of course, although it does prompt recall of the various instances of wilful damage at the French Shore sites.

'Are we safe in assuming they are all attributable to Jake?'

'You mean, are there gaps that need our combined and cunning attention?' she says. Not buoyant, but close. It's amazing the difference that can come from the distraction of a good meal when you're gut-foundered.

I'm on speakerphone to Joan in Conche. Once we get past the partial but nevertheless much-appreciated story of what unfolded over the last few hours, my question to her is simple.

'The plexiglass that was marked up—what part of the tapestry was it covering exactly?'

'The Vikings. In L'Anse aux Meadows.'

Mae and I glance at each other. Not that it came as a surprise.

'What specific part?'

'The fellow with the long blond hair cutting down a tree. Whatever idiot did it used the marker to circle his upper body together with the axe. Round and around, several times in fact.'

Definitely out to make a point. 'Anything else?' Mae inserts. 'Any words?'

'No words. Just an arrow, pointing up, under the circle. Which made no sense. It was not as if anyone could miss seeing it.'

It's only after we've said our protracted goodbyes that we verbalize what we've both been thinking—the same arrow was on the fence pickets in Croque.

'I'm assuming it's more than just an arrow,' Mae says.

'That makes two of us.' The smile comes with a wink and a nod.

'Possibly a Viking symbol of some sort.'

'You mean like a rune?'

Why hadn't we thought of that before? I whip out the phone again and it's back to Google.

'Holy shit.' It cuts the anticipation. 'Symbol of the Norse god of war, Tyr. And get this—"Rune of the balance and justice ruled from a higher rationality. The rune of sacrifice of the individual for well-being of the whole."'

'Whoa.'

'Holy shit!' Louder, this time. 'And get this—it's the symbol of the neo-Nazi Nordic Resistance Movement.'

'Whoa.'

Whoa is right.

I go back to the chart of runes and scan it again. Sure enough, there it is. No surprise. No expletive necessary.

'That engraving on the rock face, under the French ship names, what we thought was the branches of a tree—actually antlers of an elk, a sacred animal in Norse mythology. Algiz, quote, "represents protection, defence, and prosperity."'

'That gold engraving on the wristband, what you thought was a stylized "n"?'

It doesn't take long.

'Uruz.'

She's being patient. The interpretation goes on and on. It's a very manly rune, by the sound of it.

'Are you ready for this? "Overall, Uruz refers to great strength, sexuality, athleticism, virility . . . It may also indicate that subtlety and inaction are poor choices . . ."'

Mae takes her time. 'I'll try to be objective, but it sounds to me like a lot of pent-up sexual energy. Which he can't control.'

You could say that. Not sure I would.

'Early 20s. If memory serves me well . . . a lot of testosterone on the move. Maybe not so abnormal.'

She doesn't flinch. 'Regardless, he wasn't prepared for Amanda. She wasn't about to put up with his bullshit. Or with Marco's.'

Maybe "bullshit" is not quite the best term. I won't go there.

But it does shift our attention to Marco. Whom we seem to have put aside when he should be equally in the picture. There are several central questions, all still unanswered.

'Did Marco and Jake come together by happenstance,' Mae asks. 'Or were they allies beforehand? Could they have found each other on some extremist website, made plans to meet up and, after the lighthouse tour ended, carry out the stunt at L'Anse aux Meadows?'

'Either way, Amanda's presence threw off the balance. To put it mildly.'

'Why go on the tour at all? Why not just come straight to L'Anse aux Meadows?'

'He's a keener for lighthouses. I know that for a fact. Maybe he was out to kill two birds with one stone—get his lighthouse buzz and get his Viking rocks off at the same time.'

I'm tired. We both are. I just want to pick up Gaffer, get back to our hotel room, have a Scotch, settle into bed and, eventually, call it a night.

The evening doesn't unfold as planned. We show up back at Ruth's. She and Gaffer meet us at the door. The dog appears to have gotten the five-star treatment.

Notwithstanding a new development: Ruth has company. The vehicle in the driveway belongs to another person seeking particulars on Jake Moe, who, together with Marco, is now (we assume) no longer simply detained, but under arrest for suspicion of murder. And, rather beside the point, unlawful assembly.

I expect to meet an overwhelmed Colin Baxter. Not so. He appears to be placidly unaware of what has taken place at L'Anse aux Meadows. I'm not sure I should be the one to tell him. Better he hear it first from the RCMP.

At the moment he is sitting on the sofa in the living room. Given the bottle and two glasses of wine resting on the coffee table, I can only assume Ruth had been occupying the space next to him. He stands up quickly when we enter and extends his hand.

'Sebastian.'

'Mr. Baxter.' We've had intense phone conversation, but I'm not sure it puts us on a first-name basis. I introduce Mae.

'Please, call me Colin.'

He has noticed that I noticed the placement of the wine glasses. 'Ruth and I have been friends for some time, you may be surprised to know.'

Correct. I realize St. Anthony is a small town, but all the same, Ruth has no roots here. She's an occasional visitor.

'We go way back. In fact, Colin was the reason I first came to St. Anthony.'

A bit more of an explanation would be helpful, not that we should necessarily expect it.

'Colin was of great help to me after my husband passed away,' Ruth adds, reluctantly perhaps, but not without a measure of fondness for the memory it stirs.

I see. An old flame rekindled in the wake of personal upset? Not uncommon. It does, however, prompt another question.

'I'm curious, Colin, as to what brought you to St. Anthony. From Ontario, I assume.'

'I know. Not your average scenario. To go from downtown Toronto to the northern tip of Newfoundland. Let's just say I was on reset.'

Reset? I'm not meant to have a supplementary question.

'Can I get you both a glass of wine?' Ruth inserts. 'Colin brought an exceptional Niagara Chardonnay.'

I'd be surprised if the NLC in St. Anthony stocks such a thing. Colin imports it, is my guess.

'That would be lovely, Ruth. Thank you.' Mae smiles her approval.

Sooo, we're lounging around drinking Niagara Chardonnay (exceptional it is) while Colin's client, Marco (the vigilante Viking hasn't been in touch yet) is confined to a prisoner-issue chair, drinking lukewarm tap water from a plastic cup. Where do we go from here?

Of course, because of client confidentiality, we're not about to learn much—if anything—new about Marco. Colin is the one asking the questions.

'Is there anything, anything at all, you've discovered about Jake that I should be aware of, now that we know the two of them escaped confinement together. I have some suspicion they knew each other beforehand.'

A suspicion that resulted from his questioning of Marco, I assume.

Ruth would have told him of our trip to see Album Rock. It's as good a place as any to start. But that, of course, requires the backstory of the other acts of vandalism on historic properties and how our suspicions about Jake's involvement intensified.

Colin is incredulous. 'Leading you to . . . ?'

'L'Anse aux Meadows.' Out it mushrooms, the full account, in all its surreal detail. So much for getting it first from the Mounties.

'Good God,' declares Ruth. 'There was no indication whatsoever that anything like that was fomenting under this roof.'

Colin turns quickly to her. 'Are you sure? Was there anything besides the journal that caught your attention?'

Ruth has filled him in on the raunchy side of Jake's personality. But is there something to confirm the racist side?

She glances at me. 'I couldn't help but notice the wristbands. The police showed me a picture. I confirmed that was the one, like the one you just mentioned, Sebastian. But to be honest, I didn't pay it much attention at the time. And as for the tattoos, they all have them these days. Can't say I ever laid my eyes on his bare chest. His exposure, as interesting as it might have been, was limited.'

A pause, a slight smile.

'There was a black tank top he liked to wear. There was one tattoo that I *did* notice. I liked it, in fact, the way all these curves were intertwined. On his upper arm.'

'On his bicep?' Which we didn't see at L'Anse aux Meadows because of the animal skin over his shoulders.

'I prefer upper arm. Bicep makes me think of oiled-up body builders.'

Jittery laughter. A positive release for us all.

In the meantime, I've googled "Viking tattoos."

'That's it,' Ruth says when I show her the screen. 'That's the one.'

'The Horns of Odin. Three interlocking horns used sometimes, and I quote, "to symbolize the sacrifice to be made for wisdom." Whatever that might mean.' I pass the phone to the others.

Mae is taken by the variations in design. 'Tattoo artists are having a field day.' She hands me back the phone. I continue scrolling.

'The Horns of Odin tattooed on his pythons.' I catch Ruth's eye. 'As they're also known, in gym jargon, apparently. Google never fails to surprise me with the connections it spews forth that have nothing to do with your search terms.

'Now I get it,' says Ruth, with fresh excitement. '*Pythons, the Full Monty.* The words on his T-shirt. And I was thinking it was a hopeless pun on Monty Python. Goes to show you just how out of the loop I am.'

No need to go that far, Ruth. It was not an illogical conclusion.

'That black tank top he wore. Did it have any text printed on it?' asks Colin. He thinks he's on to something.

'As a matter of fact . . . I rather liked it. It said: "Don't waste your time looking back. You're not going that way."'

Her eyes are on Colin. Accompanied by the mere hint of a smile. Subtle, but, to my mind, weighty.

How about a refill on the wine, folks, to get our minds back on track? In the meantime, I'm once again on the search engine of choice. Within seconds I hit another jackpot.

'Just listen to this. The words are attributed to Ragnar Lothbrok, ninth-century Viking king. Quote: "Fearless leader and unstoppable warrior." Quote: "Scourge of Medieval England and France." Quote: "Brutal and unforgettable."'

'Never heard of him,' says Ruth. We all agree.

Except for Colin. He's chuckling. 'You *are* out of the loop. Never watched *Vikings* on Amazon Prime? Six full seasons. Ragnar Lothbrok is the main character.'

We're not responding.

'Father of Ivar the Boneless?' Interesting handle, but no takers.

'Father of Björn Ironside?' Struck out again.

So that's how small-town lawyers spend their off-hours.

On that note, we seem to have come to the end of our usefulness to Colin, as far as his interest in Jake is concerned. Jake has not shaped up to be anyone about to generate much sympathy in the eyes of a jury.

Likewise Marco. Colin has questions about him, of course. Besides what I witnessed in L'Anse aux Meadows, there's not much more to tell about Marco. Other than his sexual exploits.

Colin latches on.

'I have no way of knowing for sure,' I caution, 'what transpired between Marco and Amanda overnight at the B & B.'

'Could she have led him on, then denied him what he wanted?'

A delicate way of putting it.

'You mean enough that he wanted to seek revenge?'

'He likely went to the lighthouse, don't you think?'

'I don't think there's any doubt about that at this point.'

Colin is tossing out questions in the hope of expanding the possibilities of what actually took place. He knows full well that I don't have definitive answers, but nonetheless seems to deem it a worthwhile strategy. Let's face it, I'm the only one he knows who has had extended direct contact with Marco.

'I'll say this much. From what I saw, Marco had a general, ongoing gripe with what the world had handed him. Something in his background, something in his family life— who knows where it came from? Yet he found something in lighthouses that he valued, that satisfied him. And I think at times even brought him a measure of happiness, as elusive as that might have been.'

Colin takes a moment. 'And in a sense perhaps Amanda defiled that, by the fact that she had no real appreciation of lighthouses. To her, being there was a job, something to get past and move on.'

'Which especially irked him because she was given access to the Point Amour lighthouse in a way that he wasn't.'

'Plus the complication of whatever went on between them at the B & B,' says Colin.

'At one point, I was thinking Jake was pissed off at Marco because he had made a move on Amanda, that they were fighting over her on the catwalk. But the more I think about it, the more I suspect their relationships with Amanda only strengthened the bond between them.'

'There's a well-known link between misogyny and white supremacy,' Mae adds firmly.

Colin and I might be thinking it, but she wants to be sure it's embedded in our consciousness. It is now.

'Agreed.' Beyond that, I don't know enough to expand any discussion. As for Colin, he'll have to decide how to deal with it as he mounts a defence for his client.

The time has come for us to collect Gaffer and move out.

Colin has my contact information. He's sure to be back in touch before long.

Ruth has been left with a lot to deal with on her own. The project she worked so hard to put in place has been struck an unimaginable blow. I hope she can salvage it. She has Colin, if I'm reading the wine glasses correctly. That's the positive.

Gaffer is reluctant to depart, which thoroughly pleases his new-found friend. She bends over to pat his head, and he licks her fondly. We each have but a hug to offer, although Mae disengages once only to hug her a second time. Hopefully, Ruth feels the support.

We drive away knowing that, unlike the twosome we left behind, we can, to some extent at least, put the turmoil of the last couple of days behind us. Tomorrow we head home to St. John's.

Not before one final stop. Corporal Larsen has agreed to make it early in the morning. We'll need to get on the road. It's a twelve-hour drive to St. John's.

St. Anthony is blessed with the only Tim Hortons on the Great Northern Peninsula, situated very conveniently on the same street as the RCMP detachment. It's our breakfast stop. Followed by extra coffees to go and a one-minute drive to the parking area outside the police station.

Corporal Larsen has been given a temporary space for our heart-to-heart. We don't encounter them, but I suspect that Jake and Marco are somewhere in the building, likely under the grudgingly vigilant eye of Corporal Beauchamp.

The coffee is a gesture of goodwill. Duly acknowledged by Larsen, but he sets the cardboard tray on a table outside the room. The coffee will have to wait. The corporal has but one focus.

Our purpose in being here is to give him every last detail that is in any way related to the two prisoners about to be formally charged. Larsen has taken one of two chairs behind the desk, which leads me to assume we are about to be joined by Inspector Lockwood. Larsen opens a notebook to a pair of blank pages. Superfluous, of course, given that whatever we say will be taped.

There's a short tap on the door and when I glance behind me, the officer has already entered the room.

'Sebastian,' she says. 'Good to see you again. And Mae. We haven't met, but I've heard about you from Inspector Olsen of the RNC.' The two women shake hands.

'I'm very pleased to meet you.'

She takes the other seat behind the desk. My breath is deep and exhausting. Inspector Bowmore—top dog of RCMP criminal investigations, flown in from St. John's to take over the case. In light of the new developments, one can only assume, the junior canine has been forced aside to make way for her.

I should not be in the least disparaging. Inspector Bowmore is exceptionally good at her job, as past encounters on other cases have demonstrated. She sometimes works with Olsen, whom Mae knows as the partner of my ex-wife, Samantha. What Mae doesn't know (and I have no intention whatsoever of ever telling her) is anything about our personal history. Well in the past, I will add. And, as much as is possible, forgotten about.

It takes considerable effort, but any awkwardness on my part is firmly suppressed.

'Welcome, Inspector Bowmore. How's the weather in St. John's?'

'Not quite summer but getting there. Finally.'

'That's good. We'll find out tomorrow.' I'm upbeat. The ball is in her court.

'Corporal Larsen has briefed me on yesterday's developments. I'd like to start with how you both came to be at L'Anse aux Meadows just shortly after the two escapees showed up there. As you are aware, you arrived even before our officers did. I'll be frank—were you tipped off?'

Only by our own ingenuity. I look to the officer beside her.

'I assume Inspector Bowmore has not . . . but, Corporal Larsen, have you ever heard of Album Rock?'

No, he hasn't. As I suspected. We give them both a quick summary of its history, jumping to what we discovered and the Norwegian connection. That's the vital part, of course, linking Jake to the site and how that led us to connecting him to the Ingstads. And, of course, L'Anse aux Meadows.

It takes a while. Then there's the tattoos and the runes and all that. The corporal's note-taking can't keep up. He abandons it partway through. By the time we've concluded our storylines,

both officers can't be anything but impressed, though they're
doing their best not to show it. Mae and I have tied more than
a few ends together. Inspector Bowmore sits back in her chair.

'I don't know about you, but I could use some coffee. Did
I notice some outside the door?'

Larsen stands up, heads to the waiting tray and proceeds
to hand us each a cup, plus cream and sugar as needed. He
doctors his own and sits behind the desk again. No one cares to
mention that the coffee is a bit on the cold side.

Mae opens her tote bag and withdraws part two of our
goodwill gesture—a small selection of pastries. She opted for
croissants and Danishes, to avoid the donut/cop stereotype.
They circulate as Inspector Bowmore begins again.

'Correct me if I'm wrong . . .' A slight but significant change
of tone. 'What you're about to say, I'm assuming, is that Jake
and Marco met up at the Point Amour lighthouse and together
encountered Amanda. That she left the entrance unlocked for
one of them, most likely Jake, not realizing that the two of them
together would make their way to the catwalk.'

'That, to our minds, is a logical scenario, given they had
planned for some time to join forces and pull their stunt at
L'Anse aux Meadows.'

'And, in fact, it may have been their first actual encounter,
since their relationship likely started online and continued that
way for several months prior to Marco undertaking his trip to
Newfoundland and Labrador? Is that your thinking?'

I glance at Mae before answering. She nods. 'That is what
we've concluded.'

'In which case Amanda being part of the scene was inci-
dental.'

'Yes.'

'And would you go so far as to say that neither one of them
had any intention of pushing her over the railing to her death?'

I glance again at Mae.

'Yes,' she says, 'that's our belief.'

'That one of them, or both of them together, struggled with her and pushed her over accidently?'

'Or she fell of her own accord. Bearing in mind the position of the body after the fall.'

'Suicide?'

'Or she knowingly did nothing to stay clear of the railing. Possibly provoked a confrontation and opened herself up to the possibility of falling. Perhaps intentionally making it look like one of the two others on the catwalk, or both, pushed her to her death.'

It takes the inspector a moment to take it in.

'That's a very big assumption.'

'And not easily proven. It depends in part on what forensics concludes. And I would say more on what unfolds in the courtroom.'

'That puts a lot in the hands of their lawyer.'

'*Lawyers*, it would appear. Jake's father has the resources, presumably.'

Inspector Bowmore looks over at Corporal Larsen.

'I forgot to mention it,' Larsen says to her. He scratches a few words on a blank page of his notebook and passes it along for her to read. The name of the law firm I assume.

'Really,' she says. Impressed, it would seem.

The names of a couple of high-profile criminal lawyers in St. John's come to mind. Very possible, if money is no consideration.

'Might I add some additional thoughts?'

The inspector looks at me. She hesitates, though not for long.

'Please.'

My approval level seems to have risen.

'There needs to be more focus on Amanda—her background, what had gone on in her life up to the point she arrived to start work on the project. I had limited contact with her, but even at that I found her to be an enigma. There seemed to me to be something going on behind the scenes. I can't speculate as to what, but it absolutely needs to be investigated.'

'It's something you're doing, I assume,' says the inspector.

'Not really,' I tell her. She waits for more. 'Marco and I have reached the end of the road.'

'Amanda's mother lives in St. John's, I understand.'

'And is easy enough to contact, I would assume.' Bold of me, I realize. Making it a good point at which to expect the meeting to come to its conclusion. Inspector Bowmore has nothing more to add. I take the initiative and stand up, as does Mae. I look at Corporal Larsen.

'I assume I no longer need to remain in the area.'

Larsen glances at the inspector.

She answers for him. 'I have your contact information,' she says, unnecessarily. 'Don't be surprised if I call.'

'Of course.' I try to sound deferential. It doesn't last long. 'I would like to speak with Marco before we go. If you don't mind.'

Larsen again looks at the officer in charge. She eventually nods. They both stand up.

I'm left alone in the room. I stand by the window, giving more thought to what I will say.

Ten minutes later Marco walks in, escorted by Corporal Beauchamp.

'Knock on the door when you're finished,' Beauchamp tells me. 'I'll be just outside.' He leaves, closing the door behind him.

Marco is no longer the tour participant, no longer a suspect in need of help to save his ass. He's now an accused person, an inmate about to be formally charged with murder. He stands there, looking thoroughly aggravated.

There's no need for preamble. I get straight to the point.

'Marco, I've come to the conclusion I'm no longer of any help to you. I spoke with your lawyer. You're in good hands.'

'Fine.'

I wasn't expecting that, to be honest.

'I'm better off without you. You don't believe me anyway.' He glares at me.

'Regardless of what you think . . .'

'You have no interest in getting at the truth because you fuckin' despise me for who I am. You fuckin' think I deserve whatever the fuck happens to me, no matter if it's fuckin' justified or not.'

'You're overreacting.'

'Send me your fuckin' bill. I'm done with you.'

He heads to the door and hauls it open. Puts himself in the hands of a startled Beauchamp. Walks off with him and doesn't look back.

That was a show and a half.

Fine. That's the end of that. No more of that shit to deal with.

Fuck.

LIGHT AT THE END OF THE TUNNEL

THE DRIVE TO St. John's is endless. Neither of us has much interest in small talk, nor in discussing the situation we left behind. We're desperate to unwind and decompress.

As for Gaffer, after his time with Ruth, the Durango's rating has bottomed out completely. Still, we're expecting the poor mutt to endure the longest stretch yet of vehicular confinement. We try to talk him into chilling out, with no success. We try treats, but that can only be a stopgap measure. Finding some place to turn off the highway every hour for a dog walk and playtime is out of the question.

Mae suddenly remembers reading that music has a calming effect on dogs. Not the lighthouse compilation for sure. Both man and dog have had more than enough of that. I'm thinking Gregorian chant. Mae's searching the internet for playlists. We're desperate.

'Here we go. The canine music of choice for road trips— soft rock and reggae. Avoid Led Zeppelin and Metallica. Choose the Eagles and Bob Marley. At the top of the list: "How Deep Is Your Love" by the Bee Gees.'

And yes, "Desperado" just about sums it up. We'll try any-thing. Gaffer, my boy, as Bryan Adams (coming in at number three on the list) would say, "(Everything I Do) I Do It for You."

The Durango's media options are exceptional. Once we've worked our way through the suggested playlist, our minds now suitably programmed, we veer into our own choices. A lot of James Taylor and Diana Krall. Gaffer's personal favourite turns out to be Elton John. Most especially, "Rocket Man (I Think It's Going to Be a Long, Long Time)." I swear that dog has a sense of humour.

Indeed, by the time "Don't Let the Sun Go Down on Me" makes it into the mix, we've turned off the TCH and are heading into downtown St. John's. We've dropped a tired Mae at her abode, made a quick (and rewarding) NLC stop, and find ourselves on Military Road, pulling up to our very own sanctuary of choice. We're closing in on nine p.m.

'Siri, what's the official sunset time for today in St. John's, Newfoundland?'

'Sunset will be 9:02 p.m. today.'

A celebratory release of Gaffer from confinement and onto the sidewalk. Then directly across the road to Government House grounds, the parkland where Gaffer roves and romps and discreetly does his business. Oh, the joy.

For me, the joy is the comfy chair and a robust dram of Talisker Storm. Powerful and Smoky. Brooding Spice. Made by the Sea. (One of the two bottles remaining in the city. Right on!)

When the bedside light goes out, me under the covers and Gaffer on top of them, we're knackered. It's been a very long day. Unfortunately, I don't drop away to sleep in the way I expected. It seems the consoling effect of the Scotch will only go so far, ultimately unable to contain all the strands of conversation still on the loose in this head of mine.

Which ring loudest? Those of Marco, undoubtedly.

And just what the hell will I do about that?

The morning brings the drop-off of the stalwart Durango and then the reunion with Nick. The lad has started his job. Waitering seems to be a good fit—thanks in no small way, I will add, to the fact he and I have been making meals together from scratch for years. Plus, we all know he can be a charmer when the conversation calls for it. A smart, six-foot, good-looking seventeen-year-old—it works on a lot of levels. As the tips he's been getting confirm. Welcome to the world of free enterprise.

He's got news. 'You won't believe this, but guess what band is playing St. John's in August?'

Likely someone famous to him, but unknown to me.

Nick can't wait. 'The Lumineers!'

'No kidding.' Which means I've heard of them. I'm not totally out of it.

'Remember that song on the playlist—"In the Light"?'

Right. That's where I've heard of them. One of Nick's choices. I rather liked it actually.

'I mean—what are the chances? The perfect tie-in to the tour. *Lumin*—light. Get it—*Right On! Light On!* The Lumineers!'

I get it.

'Very cool.' Although I can't work myself up to his level of excitement.

'Kofi and I got tickets already.'

So much for saving his hard-earned money for university. 'Who else is playing?' As in someone I might not need a prompt to recognize.

'On the second night—Alanis Morissette.'

'Wow. Really?'

'A bit before my time.'

But not mine. Or Mae's. Mae once told me "Jagged Little Pill" defined her later adolescence. Guess what tickets we'll be buying.

It's a relief to have my head around something other than the madness that went on in Point Amour.

The return to near normal doesn't last long, unfortunately. Second only to Nick's excitement about the Lumineers is his need to know about what transpired after he boarded the bus in Deer Lake.

'Are you serious? No way. Holy crap!' That sums up his reaction.

I leave the sore point to the end.

'I'm not totally surprised,' Nick says. 'There was something about Marco. Remember I was in the rear of the vehicle while you were driving. I saw plenty of him. He mostly kept to himself. Spent a lot of time on his phone. I figured porn, but I can only guess what else. He was likely a good candidate for indoctrination.'

'Why do you say that?'

'I don't think he had much of a life as a kid. He said to me once—your dad and you, you really like each other a lot. I told him yeah, we do. He said, lucky you. That was all—but, you know, I figure that said quite a bit.'

'You think he was looking for something that was missing in his life? From what I read, a lot of these guys grow up alienated.'

'They band together to find acceptance. It empowers them, I guess.'

That's only part of the picture. The bigger half is the death of Amanda Thomsen. 'What about murder? Do you think she was a candidate for murder?'

Pretty blunt, I know. Nick isn't prepared for it. He hesitates, working up an answer.

'I already told you what I thought. Amanda had significant hang-ups.'

'I remember.'

'I haven't changed my mind.'

'You figure it threw Marco off, but not enough that he would push her over the railing?'

Nick looks intently at me.

'You're putting words in my mouth. What I'm saying is that someone needs to find out more about Amanda. If you want to drop Marco, that's up to you. But you can't go around wondering if you made the right decision. You have to be satisfied that his lawyer or the cops are doing the job you would have done.'

That about sums it up. He's right. Of course. And I should at least admit it.

As his father, I could, I suppose, take some satisfaction from knowing that a kid I raised might just turn out to be smarter than I am.

There's one other individual who could offer a perspective that might be of help. In one way or another, the fellow in question— an inspector with the Royal Newfoundland Constabulary—has been involved in all the murder investigations I've been part of. I'd be the first to admit he's taught me a few things over the years, but this time, I've been more than a little stoked at handling the whole business myself, without him looming over my shoulder. Given the fact that he just happens to be the live-in of my ex-wife, having him out of the picture has done me a lot of good. Until now. I'm quite capable of putting pride aside in favour of purposeful advice.

I don't assume for a second that Inspector Frederick Olsen of the RNC is unaware of what I've been up to. Nick is resident in the same house, when he's not with me, and then there's his good friend and occasional colleague Ailsa Bowmore, the RCMP inspector I toughed it out with in St. Anthony a mere two days ago.

'Fred, it's Sebastian. How you doin'?'

'Good. More to the point, how are *you* doing?'

If he's surprised to hear from me, it doesn't sound like it.

'Excellent.' Keeping my cool at all costs. The cop in him instinctively seeks the lead.

'Fred, you heard about what happened in Labrador, at the lighthouse?'

'It's been all over the news. And the business at L'Anse aux Meadows. There was an eyewitness report in the newspaper. Her story even made it to the *Guardian*.'

'No kidding.'

'Picture and all. I thought that might have been you and Mae in the crowd of people in the foreground. Hard to tell. Everyone was back on to the camera, except for the accused.'

'They've been formally charged, I take it.'

'You didn't know?'

'Just not officially.' Obviously, I don't have Inspector Bowmore behind the scenes pumping me with information. Not a great start. Nevertheless, let's move on.

'Fred, I have a couple of questions.'

'Fire away.'

No need to sound that enthusiastic. I bend over backwards trying not to see it as satisfaction at the thought that I couldn't do without his input.

It takes several minutes to churn out the details of the case as I experienced them. He might not think it, but Olsen needs more than a cop's take on what happened, if he's going to be of any help. When he's suitably prepped, I lay out what for me has now become my core debate.

'Given I'm no longer on anyone's payroll, what's likely to

happen if your average Joe starts asking questions, to see where it gets him?'

'There's no law against asking questions. But is anyone going to answer them if you have no official role in the investigation? Isn't that the first question Amanda's mother will put to you—who are you to be asking me this? Especially given that she might not want to be talking about it in the first place.'

I don't deny it—if there's anyone who has the answers to the questions about Amanda, it's her mother. Besides which, she's the only connection to Amanda whom I know about at the moment. Who knows where her answers, if I ever get to that stage, might lead?

'Your uniform opens doors,' I tell him. 'What I have is a plastic card in a wallet.'

'A licence, but no employer. Just be careful. You don't want to be getting in the way of the RCMP. If both of you are ringing her doorbell, you're likely to be the one to lose out.'

'I have no way of knowing what the Mounties are up to.'

Olsen might know, but he's not about to tell me if he does. Police confidentiality, never mind what good it does.

'It's a case of now or never.' To be as blunt as I can be about it without an expletive.

'If you want to look at it that way,' he says.

'Any other suggestions?'

'You could step back. Put it out of your mind and let the RCMP do their job.'

I could.

But then again, more than likely I won't.

TURN THE LIGHTS OUT
WHEN YOU LEAVE

GIVEN MY LIMITED resources, I have no luck tracking down an address for Amanda's mother, whose full name I remember from a breakfast conversation with Peggy at the B & B in Forteau—Astrid Thomsen. Formerly little Asti Buckle, according to Cecil in West St. Modeste.

The next course of action is to contact Colin Baxter. I break the ice by asking if he's heard anything about a report from forensics.

'Nothing. You know the cops. They take their time. They know a lot rests on whatever they conclude.'

I move on. Of the people who might have had contact with Amanda's mother when she reached Forteau, Colin is my best bet. There's no point in going to the police, now that I'm back to being your average Joe.

'Sorry,' the lawyer tells me. 'No address at this point.'

Not good. But there's some hope.

'I did see her. Briefly, when she arrived in Forteau. She was still quite upset. There was no way she was going to talk to me about Amanda. I couldn't push it, as much as I need

to if I'm going to get more of a background on her daughter.
I've been thinking about what you said. You're right, about
digging into Amanda's past. When things settle down, I'll
phone. The RCMP will have her mother's contact info.'

And be willing to release it to a lawyer for the defence.

'So you think a phone call will be enough?'

'It'll have to be, for now. At this point I can't see myself
coming all the way into St. John's on spec. I'll see what develops.'

I might as well come out and say it.

'How about I talk to her on your behalf?'

A distinct pause.

'You mean I hire you? I'm not sure I have . . .'

'In name only. No cost.'

'I doubt that's legitimate.'

'We'll make it legitimate. Listen, what Amanda's mother
can tell us could very well prove crucial. She could be the key
to your whole defence.'

There's no response. Probably because he figures I've over-
stepped any boundaries that exist between us. That, or he thinks
it's reached the point I'm no longer any worth to him.

'Sebastian, I'm not comfortable with this. I'll do my job,
you do what you feel you have to.'

Enough beating around the bush.

'You'll be expecting me to tell you anything I find out that
might be useful to the defence. Am I right? In which case, if
Marco's ass is going to be saved, or Jake's for that matter, then
we need to pull out all the stops. Maybe we find nothing.
Maybe they are guilty. Maybe one or both of them together
pushed Amanda over the damn railing. But if we try, and find
nothing, at least we know. At least we get to call it a day with a
clear conscience. And get to fuckin' sleep at night.'

That's it. I've said all I'm going to say. I wait. He's working
up some response, whatever the hell it might be.

'A bottle of Laphroaig 25 Year Old. Cask strength.'

Now what the . . .?

'That's your fee. That's what I'll pay you. If you find anything that makes a difference.'

I can't help but chuckle. And shake my bloody head.

'Done deal.'

'When I find out where she's living, I'll let you know.'

Astrid Thomsen lives in a much-sought-after section of St. John's called Churchill Park. There's a bronze bust of Winston in the green space not far from her house, although, unfortunately, it's a regular target of low-flying birds. Nonetheless, the general area is prime real estate, dating back to the mid-1940s. It's one of the very first planned suburbs in Canada from that era. I know it well, as does Gaffer. Very nicely designed, with a system of connecting dog-friendly pathways, most of which still exist, except for the few that some myopic landowners talked equally myopic city officials into eliminating.

Her street is quiet, ending in a cul-de-sac. Lots of mature trees, all the properties well taken care of. As we approach the house and park the car on the street, I see it's one of the more modest homes. Most of the others have been renovated to something much bigger than the originals.

Astrid, I see, is an accomplished gardener. Her hostas are showpieces.

'No doubt she knows when to deadhead,' says Mae. 'The insignificant flowers die off, leaving these ugly scapes. A true hosta lover is all about the foliage, not the flowers.'

Which only goes to show just how far Mae has come since her adolescence. (I will add that she was absolutely thrilled when we snapped up tickets to see Alanis Morissette.)

Shift of focus to the front door. We pause for a few seconds before heading up the driveway. We are deliberately arriving unannounced. I'm thinking I'll be less likely to be cut off in mid-sentence than if I'd phoned. I'm counting on a minute or two for the persuasive words that might get us an invitation inside.

I ring the bell and stand back next to Mae, so Astrid Thomsen will have a clear view of the unintimidating couple.

I'm considering ringing a second time when the door opens and before us stands a tall, well-dressed woman in a subtle polka-dot dress and leggings, her shoulders covered by a cotton shawl. Yet unsmiling and ready to become impatient if need be.

'I'm sorry, I'm not really interested,' she says. 'I have my own affiliation. Thank you.'

I think she's mistaken us for Jehovah's Witnesses. It's clear we've dressed too conservatively.

'My name is Sebastian Synard. I'm so very sorry for the passing of your daughter. I'm the person who discovered Amanda after her fall at the lighthouse.' It's as gentle as I can make it.

She's taken aback, of course, and suddenly close to tears. I introduce Mae.

'I'm very sorry,' Mae says. 'I can't imagine how difficult it is for you.'

'I knew Amanda briefly,' I tell her. 'We were staying at the same B & B in Forteau.'

'You're the tour guide.'

'Yes, that's right.' Revealed at some point in her conversations with Corporal Larsen I assume.

'Who also happens to be a private detective.'

Not where I want to be going at this point.

'Yes, I am,' adding quickly, 'but I've come by because I thought sharing my recollections of Amanda might be helpful to you in dealing with the tragedy. May we come in?'

Not the whole truth, and she senses it. 'Has someone hired you?'

There's no avoiding it.

'I've been asked by Colin Baxter, the defence lawyer, to help with the investigation. Mr. Baxter thought that by speaking with you, since I spent a considerable amount of time with his client, it might help clarify what led to the tragedy. I think clarity is something we are all striving for.'

Somewhat vague on my part, and not entirely making sense, but I'm betting on the suggestion of clarity. She, no doubt, has had difficulty coming to terms with what's happened. Clarification, no matter where it's coming from, would likely be appreciated.

'It won't take long,' Mae assures her. 'If it reaches the point that you'd rather we leave, just tell us.'

Astrid Thomsen is confused and unsure how to respond. But I believe she has been left alone with her grief for her daughter and is desperate to talk about what happened, especially to someone so closely tied to what took place.

In the end, and with some reluctance, she agrees.

Her sitting room is noticeably restrained. Several levels up from IKEA, but still rather minimalistic. The walls are pewter grey, the sofa and matching armchair off-white. An area rug of subtle geometric design is centred on light hardwood. Framed black-and-white photographs rest on floating shelves. An overhead lighting fixture looks like an inverted tree limb. Lots of white candles.

It is not the time to discuss decor, however. We all have minds that need settling. I move past the condolences to place myself directly in line with the events leading up to the tragedy.

'I had breakfast with Amanda that morning, before she set off for the day. I found her to be somewhat agitated. In retrospect, I wonder why. If you don't mind me asking, had you been in recent contact with her and could you suggest a possible reason for her agitation? I think that will help us understand her frame of mind as she went about her day.'

She wasn't expecting me to be so direct. It's risky, I realize. She hesitates but answers.

'Amanda phoned the day before. She had been in a relationship that ended.'

'With Jake Moe, I understand.'

'She was concerned how the two of them would deal with the fact they still had to work together.'

'From what I gather,' says Mae, 'she was a strong young woman. Would I be right in saying she had the resilience to deal with it?'

'Perhaps less so since her father passed away. They were very close.'

I think it better not to be getting into the circumstances of her father's death, at this point at least.

'He was the reason Amanda took up photography. Her father came to Newfoundland to work in the oil industry, but photography was his lifelong passion.'

'These are some of his photographs?' I ask, looking around the room.

'Yes. And Amanda's.'

I did notice, when I entered the room, that a few photographs were partial nudes. Bare female limbs, somewhat in shadow. Surprising, I thought, for a sitting room. Even more surprising, now that I know who was behind the camera. Or maybe I'm just out of sync with social norms these days. It wouldn't be the first time.

'Amanda struck me as self-possessed,' I say to her mother. 'Very confident in her abilities as a photographer.'

If our conversation sounds stilted, it's because it is. I don't know the woman and we're into personal territory. I don't think it can be otherwise.

'I'm not surprised she struck you that way. She did have her insecurities, as we all did at that age.'

I stiffen even more, unsure how to get her to open up about just what those insecurities might have been. If I'm too direct, it increases the risk of being asked to leave.

'You're thinking there is a possibility of suicide?' she says.

Okay. That dilemma solved itself rather unexpectedly.

'It is something the police would have considered before laying charges,' inserts Mae, on the surface at least, more relaxed than I am.

'I discussed this with the RCMP. I was honest. Amanda has had rough periods in her life. But nothing that would ever suggest suicide.'

Her mother might well be the last to know. Perhaps Amanda had friends she talked to, other young women she confided in.

I hear what I take to be a cellphone ringtone. It's brief, a text, I assume. Astrid stands up and goes in search of the phone, into what I take to be the kitchen. She's not there long. She reappears.

'Excuse me for a moment.' She walks past the sitting room and out the front door.

Mae and I look at each other. Mae stands and ventures near the picture window. 'She's approaching someone in a car parked at the end of the driveway.'

Will I do it? I think I might have time before she returns.

'Keep me posted if she turns to come back inside.'

It's the kitchen. I look around. The phone is on the counter.

I check the screen. It displays a message from someone named Anton. *I'm still in hell over this. I see a car. Are you alone? CU46?*

I return to the sitting room. Mae is still at the window, but quickly returns to the sofa. She sits next to me.

The front door opens and Astrid rejoins us. She's upset.

'I will have to arrange to meet with you both another time. I'm sorry. I'm sure you appreciate how difficult the last several days have been.'

We have no choice but to again pass on our condolences and make our way to the door. I leave her with my card.

'Please, when you feel up to it, I would appreciate a phone call.'

'Thank you for your understanding.' She closes the door behind us.

There is no longer a vehicle parked at the end of the drive-way. 'A Mercedes, I think it was,' says Mae.

'Did you get a look at who was driving?'

'Just a glimpse, when he leaned out the window. Enough, I think, to catch a resemblance.'

'A resemblance? To whom?'

'Jake.'

'You're kidding.'

'That same high forehead. Blond hair. I could be wrong.'

'The guy in the car, he texted her. His name is Anton.'

Only then does it hit me.

'Shit.'

'What?'

'When Jake was on the phone, in the cop station, when he went ballistic about getting a lawyer, he phoned someone. Whoever it was, he called him Anton.'

'Too much of a coincidence.'

'The text said, *Are you alone? CU46?* Any idea what CU46 means? Code for something I assume.'

What text abbreviations I do know I've picked up from Nick. Anything past OMW and SYS and I'm getting into unknown territory.

We're in the car. Mae is on Google. I start the engine and check the side mirror. I pull out from the parking spot.

I'm about to turn around in the cul-de-sac at the end of the street. 'Are you ready for this?' she says.

'Go for it.'

'CU46—See you for sex.'

I pull the car to the curb and park. No distractions as I try to get my head around that.

'She's in a relationship with Jake's father, an intense one by the sound of it.'

'The creep shows up looking for sex less than a week after her daughter's funeral.'

'A death possibly caused by his son, who has been arrested on suspicion of murder.'

'It's all too weird,' says Mae.

'No wonder Amanda had issues.'

'Starting with a father who took photographs of half-nude women, which the mother has on display in her living room. Which could have been photographs of Astrid herself, for all we know.'

Really? I hadn't thought of that. At this point nothing should surprise me.

'On top of all that,' she continues, 'her lover's son turns out to be a white supremacist. Which now makes more sense, given Jake has a self-centred ass for a father. I know Anton's type. Thinks he's God's gift to women. I doubt if Astrid is the only one he's been hitting on.'

'A lot to surmise from one text.'

'I can tell a leech a mile away.'

Our conversation comes to a halt, if not the debate in Mae's mind. I pull the car into the street.

There's a need to step back. To attempt a broader view. Elements have shaped themselves into a murky picture, elements in need of scrutiny and a deeper probe. And considerable skill to help frame a defence argument in a courtroom. I don't envy

Colin Baxter, but it seems to me that it does make the scenario somewhat more promising for his client. No excusing Marco for his warped ideology, but the fellow had no idea what was about to entangle him once he teamed up with Jake.

Mae and I were planning to cook supper at my place with Nick, who has the day off from work. We're no longer sure we're up to it.

'A gin and tonic sounds very good at this point,' she says once we get there. 'And how about we order in.'

The only one who's his normal, unperturbed self is Gaffer. As for the other three, there's a lot of incredulity and speculation to go with the Filipino food from RJ Pinoy Yum. I thought the food would help put me in a frame of mind to reconnect at some point with Marco. Not to get directly involved in his defence, just to see how he's doing.

I'm spooning more scrummy chicken adobo onto my plate as I'm updating Nick.

'Then I see this text: *Are you alone? CU46.*'

'Wow. That's freaky.'

The fork doesn't quite make it to my mouth.

'You know what that means?'

The trap door has snapped quite loudly behind him.

'I don't use it, of course.'

'Of course.'

'Just heard of it.'

'Of course.' I'm tempted to add: and what do you use? But think better of it. It takes considerable restraint on my part, but let's keep going.

Nick attacks the beef caldereta with new gusto, a diversionary tactic that's rather unworldly in my estimation.

Mae steps in, appreciated by both sides. 'The questions have returned. How likely was suicide? How much of a case is there to be made for it being an accident, generated by the two reprobates being there, but involuntary nonetheless?'

'Now, at least, there's a substantial argument to be made for it.' In my opinion.

'Beyond a reasonable doubt,' quotes Nick. 'That's the standard presented to a jury. Let's not forget that the prosecution holds the burden of proof.'

The young man has partially redeemed himself. He did a research paper on Canadian criminal law for one of his high school courses. Consulted his father several times in the course of writing it, as I recall. Nonetheless, he makes a crucial point.

'There's months, maybe years, before this is resolved. The lawyers get their teeth into it and let's see where it goes.'

One more call to Colin Baxter and that's the extent of my involvement, for now. If it does go to trial, I'll be called to testify, undoubtedly. In the meantime, there's another tour to finalize.

As for the three of us around the table, there's leche flan for dessert.

'My favourite,' says Nick, smiling, although not too broadly.

The call to Colin goes as expected. He's impressed. He's intrigued.

'This is very useful, Sebastian.'

I like "useful." It smells of Laphroaig 25 Year Old.

'Let me think more about this. I should consult with Jake's lawyers before going any further. You may hear from them. And I'll have to come into St. John's at some point.'

'We'll get together.'

'Undoubtedly.'

'I'll bring along the goods.' He chuckles before saying goodbye.

Until then I'm stuck with the newly opened bottle of Talisker.

Not stuck. The Talisker's pretty much a beast. Powerful and Smoky—hitting the taste buds like the whisky gods are on fire. Brooding Spice—you're not kidding. Made by the Sea—in a raging Storm at that!

And in my other hand—*Stargazing: Memoirs of a Young Lighthouse Keeper*. Do I really want to be reading a book that will constantly evoke memories of my recent, multiple lighthouse experiences? The good, the bad, and the ugly?

No. But I will. For the sake of a good book. And the fact that I will be mulling them over anyway.

Who doesn't need to keep his lens on life well polished?

Have another enlightening dram, Sebastian, I'm thinking. It's been a tough tour.

CELESTIAL LIGHT

I CAN'T SAY I expected the phone call. But neither was I taken by surprise.

Several days ago, when we left her house, Astrid Thomsen was in an uncertain mood. The image of her retrieving my card and entering its sequence of numbers into her phone stays with me until, less than a half-hour later, I'm standing outside her door. She opens it shortly after I ring the bell.

'Please come in.'

Her hair has been drawn back loosely from her face. She is wearing a thin cardigan in quiet colours over a delicate, floral dress. If Mae was with me, I'm sure she would again be taken with Astrid's stylishness.

Mae is at work and I didn't get in touch with her. I will later. I wanted to come alone.

'Please, have a seat, Mr. Synard.'

Her voice is strained. I would not expect otherwise.

'Sebastian.'

'Astrid, then.'

It is better than the formal words, but awkward none-theless.

The living room is different. I noticed it immediately. Gone are the framed black-and-white photographs on the floating shelves. They have been replaced by others, smaller and in colour.

'Can I offer you a coffee, or tea?'

'No, thank you just the same. A glass of water would be good.'

Her time in the kitchen gives me the opportunity to look more closely at the photographs. One is undoubtedly the light-house in West St. Modeste. And the person in another looks to be Eddie, with the harbour in Croque in the background, gulls passing overhead.

'Amanda's,' she says when she returns. 'Some of the last photos she took. She would email those she particularly liked.'

Astrid sets down a coaster on the side table next to the sofa, together with the glass of water. She walks to one of the shelves and removes a photograph. She places it in my hands, then sits in an armchair directly across from me.

'Do you recognize the image?'

I hesitate to say so, but I do. Against a cloud-filled sky is the red pinnacle of a lighthouse and below it a section of what can only be part of a Fresnel lens through a lantern-room window.

'It is the last one she sent.' She struggles with the words. 'Taken not long before she died. Would you agree?'

I struggle with my response. 'She had prolonged her stay at the lighthouse to capture that image.'

'And between the moment she took the picture and the moment she died, a great deal happened.'

'Yes, it did.' I place the photograph on a coffee table nearby.

'You are wondering why I asked you here?'

There is a brief pause. 'Yes.'

'I wish to share something with you. A phone message. Amanda phoned me from the lighthouse. I was otherwise engaged. My cell was turned off.'

I am ill-prepared for this. Yet the woman is firm in her

decision to play it for me. Without any indication of what her daughter might have said.

I try to stay calm. Without success.

Astrid gathers her phone from the coffee table. She takes a little time before she initiates Amanda's voice.

Hello . . . Too bad you didn't answer. There it is . . . I assume you like the picture. It's been a long wait for the right light conditions . . . From Dad I learned patience. He used to say photography takes time, as do most good things in life. His time ran out. Faster than it should have . . I think you know one of the reasons for that.

Her voice catches. The sound of a deep breath. A sustained pause.

From you I learned confidence. While I was waiting on the light, a man appeared. I was not surprised. We enjoyed each other last evening. I had left the entrance unlocked. The idea of an encounter at this height was shamelessly tempting. So close to the heavens and all. I'm sure you understand . . .

A still longer pause. I'm expecting the call could end at any moment.

He left with the intention of seeing me later. There were a few more photographs I wanted to take . . . It hasn't worked out that way. Not long after he left, who showed up but your lover's son. He had told me he was going back to St. Anthony this afternoon . . . Jake was not in a good mood. I suspect it was his way of getting back at me. He wanted to hurt me in some way. With words, as it turned out. He was always good with words . . . Do I believe them? I wish I didn't. He said his father was having an affair with you while Dad lay in the hospital.

Amanda is crying now, though the sound of it grows fainter, as if she had set the phone away from her. Her mother raises a hand to her mouth in an effort to hold in her own tears. The return of the voice startles me.

Months in a coma from the accident was no fucking excuse. Agreed? . . . It's too late to agree . . . When Jake was leaving, I gave him the key to lock up. I told him I had another. I lied . . . Without raising the camera I snapped what I hope is a picture of the key in his hand, so you would know for certain nobody came after him. Then I was left alone . . . Which I am . . . Alone with the light. Light that will continue through the night, once the lantern room comes alive . . . I don't think I'll be here to see it . . . Do you know what Carl Jung said about light? "The sole purpose of human existence is to kindle a light in the darkness of mere being." . . . I think he lied.

Now there is silence. Astrid sets the phone back on the coffee table. She is staring at the photograph beside it. It seems she is waiting for me to speak.

'I'm very sorry.'

It is the limit of my attempt to console her.

'My husband and Anton were best friends. They came to Newfoundland together. They both had jobs with Hibernia.' Her eyes fill with tears. 'I have nothing more to do with him. It's much too late, I realize.'

She is not looking for sympathy. Yet she has lost her daughter. She is in pain and I feel the need to help her past it.

'If she had been somewhere else when she found out, it might have been different. It was such a treacherous place, so easy to allow it to happen.'

Perhaps she has also considered that. She doesn't respond. I look away.

'You're wondering why you?' she says eventually. 'Why you first, before I pass it over to the police?'

'Yes,' I admit. The thought occurs to me that it is her way of prolonging the torment for Anton, and for his son.

'I talked to Amanda that morning. She had met you the night before and the two of you had breakfast together. She told me you said something that reminded her of her father.'

I try to refocus and set my mind back. I'm not sure what I said at the time.

'Something about getting through rough times.'

I did. I remember.

She continues looking at me. 'Even if I had answered the phone that evening, I'm not sure anything I could have said would have made a difference.'

Her only consolation perhaps.

'I wanted you to know she was thinking of you. That you brought to mind her father. He meant the world to her.'

As I stand at the door to leave, I reach out and hold her hand. It's brief, supportive, but I can't say affectionate. I hope she has close friends. She is dearly in need of them, for the troubling months and years to come.

I drive back home and park the car. I don't go inside. I need a walk. A long and demanding one. I head toward Signal Hill.

The top of the hill is partially shrouded in fog. Not uncommon, although not attractive for most hikers or tourists. They have yet to realize that the fog and the light that penetrates it have their own special qualities.

I detour from the regular paths to a spot I've come to before, where I know for certain I will be alone. In the distance is Cape Spear, though I can't see it. It, too, is partially shrouded in fog.

I can see a faint flash of light from its lighthouse. The newer, taller one. The most easterly in North America. Not long ago experienced by the pharos four.

I sit on the damp grass and stare in its direction, counting the seconds between the flashes, finding some solace in its certainty.

It is true, lighthouses have an undeniable lure.

Who among us doesn't aspire to being a beacon of hope as trauma swirls about us? Who doesn't wish to be a guiding light for the newborn child who one day towers over you?

I've yet to phone Mae. I will, soon.

For now all I want to do is sit and take in the light.

ALSO IN THIS SERIES

One for the Rock
Two for the Tablelands
Three for Trinity
Four for Fogo Island

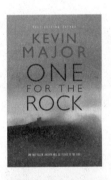